Looking for AFRICA in AMERICA

The Power of Positive Change

IKE OKWUONU

LitPrime Solutions
21250 Hawthorne Blvd
Suite 500, Torrance, CA 90503
www.litprime.com
Phone: 1-800-981-9893

Published by LitPrime Solutions   06/24/2022

ISBN: 978-1-955944-91-5(sc)
ISBN: 978-1-955944-92-2(e)

Library of Congress Control Number: 2022908770

CONTENTS

INTRODUCTION

At last, Johnson decided to tell his story about the impact of the stripping away of African American culture on him growing up in America. On a broader scope, in his opinion, the loss of his originality has affected his relationships with both blacks and whites in society. He claimed that the effects of his inherited cultural deficiency were responsible for his instability, dropping out of school, inability to keep a job, and other failures. However, according to Johnson, the purpose of this book is to externalize the behavioral power of positive change and its ability to enable him to develop ways to connect and engage with others. Johnson believes that when one achieves one's dream, the individual adds a feather to the hat of greatness.

Nicole intended to help Johnson keep a positive attitude in his relationships with fellow blacks and whites in America. She had her share of injustice from racism, prejudice, and many other unjust treatments experienced by black people in a world dominated by white people. For Johnson, he came in contact with different faces of racism, prejudice, disrespect, and double standard. He felt discriminated in school, inside churches, at work, and in other public places. His mother observed Johnson's signs of withdrawal behavior in his relationships with people, especially those who do not look like him. Nicole became worried about her son developing low self-concept as a direct impact of the injustice he experienced in the form of discrimination in establishments headed by white folks.

Melting pot. Johnson learned that the melting pot was where all the different ethnic groups were united into one big "white" ethnic group through the process of assimilation. He further learned that because every cultural value of black people was stripped away, they came into the melting pot late and empty-handed (everything black or African was bad, and everything white or European was good). He was concerned about this double standard as every other ethnic group, except African Americans, came into the melting pot with something to offer the pot. Consequently, because the African Americans were not allowed to contribute anything of their origin to the pot, Johnson had to borrow from the pot everything of cultural value that he needed for his daily functioning. Johnson believed that this omission of African values in the melting pot kept him (as an African American), other African Americans, and the big white ethnic group all continuously looking for Africa in the pot. He saw that this omission kept him working round-the-clock, searching to recover that part of himself that was missing. From Johnson's conversations with his friends Uncle Paul and Uncle Jo, Johnson concluded that he needed that part of him that was missing to be a stable, whole person. He needed to achieve this (wholeness) to relate and negotiate with individuals from other ethnic origins from the standpoint of equality, pride, and high self-concept. Johnson's awareness created an insight that he could psychotherapy himself by making a change that would involve regaining the values that his ancestors lost and passed on to him through the gene/experience process of human development. In his mind, regaining his cultural strength would help him create the optimism necessary to solve his problems: dropping out of school, being always angry and blaming other people, and instability in getting along with people in school, in the workplace, and other places of social and economic activities.

Johnson based his story on ideas from his life experiences, stories from his Great-Uncle Jo, his mother's parenting, and the answers to questions that Johnson asked his friend, a retired white man, Dr. Paul, whom Johnson also called Uncle Paul. Dr. Paul was about eighty years old and was a former psychology professor at a university.

Johnson learned later that the same white masters who stripped away the African cultural background from his ancestors later offered liberty and freedom to them. He believed that the power of liberty and freedom allowed him to reconstruct his cultural base. Johnson then decided that he would not live as his parents did. Instead, he must give up his anger and regain his cultural strength to enable him to bring closure to the "hole" in his heart. This gave him a positive feeling about white people and helped him take advantage of the opportunities in America not available elsewhere in the world. For Johnson, it was time to "find Africa" and stop the cycle of transferring negative emotions from generation to generation of his ethnic group. He believed it was time to change from being defensive to taking personal responsibility for conflicts with others around him. He saw America as the greatest country in the world, with numerous opportunities. He believed that his loss of originality prevented him from being able to take advantage of the opportunities around him in America.

Johnson traveled to Africa, regained his originality, and returned to America in his second coming. He went back to college and graduated in law with honors. He married a white lady, worked as a prosecutor, and later ran and was elected city mayor.

CHAPTER 1

Background History

Johnson acknowledged that in this world, different people tell different stories about themselves. Some people's stories reflect happy experiences, and for others, their stories may not be so joyous. Johnson talked about black/white issues as negatively experienced and his efforts toward a positive change. He grew up nurtured by his mother in the absence of his father.

Johnson was born a happy, healthy boy. To him, his world was his mother. He did not know who his father was because his mother was unwed. He was always clinging to his mother like most children of single mothers do. His mother's parents were poor, living in the inner city area in America. Johnson's mother, Nicole, and her parents lived in a small old house that her parents were renting. It was in this old house that Johnson was born. Nicole did not finish her high school education before she became pregnant. She always wondered what life would have been like if she had had enough education. Nicole would look at white people and wish that she had been born white. She believed that white girls of her age had all the good things of life—wealthy parents, better houses, fancy clothes, and money to spend. When Nicole became pregnant, her boyfriend ran away to be free from the responsibilities of raising a child. Nicole's problems increased as she had to go through the period of pregnancy without any support from her boyfriend. Johnson was born into poverty, and that was where his life started. When Johnson was about three years old, his mother lost her father. Nicole decided to move to a big city where she could use public transportation to get around.

Nicole knew that they needed government assistance. She felt that moving to a big city would make resources from the government more easily accessible to her and her family. In addition, Nicole hoped to get a job there in the city to enable her subsidized government assistance to make ends meet. In the meantime, Johnson was growing very fast. Nicole wished that Johnson would grow up to be a lawyer or a doctor. She often regretted her lack of education and resolved that she would encourage her son to be well educated. Johnson and her mother were living in a government low-income house. They were living on food stamps. When Johnson's mother needed cash urgently, she would sell some of the food stamps to enable her to buy other things they needed. She might not have known that selling food stamps is illegal. With time, Nicole found a low-income job in a factory. She would leave Johnson with his grandmother when she went to work.

As Johnson became of age for preschool, Nicole registered him for school. Johnson was very happy to get out of the house to play with other kids. But little did Johnson know that his mother intended to restrict him from having many friends, especially around their house, after school. Nicole was always thinking of what she could do to ensure that her son succeeded in life. Johnson was a smart boy in school. He was well behaved, and the teachers liked him very much. Nicole made sure that Johnson went to bed early every night. However, Johnson never liked his mother's control but became used to that with time. He never had many toys and clothes as his mother was poor. Each time Nicole went to the store with her son, they would go home with Johnson crying. He cried because his mother never allowed him to take those things when he reached out to grab toys and some food. After all, she had no money with which to pay. As time went on, Nicole stopped taking Johnson with her shopping. Then came a difficult problem—Nicole's mother took ill and passed away. She lost her best friend in the world, the only person who helped her take care of her son. Johnson cried at the passing of his grandmother because he loved her very much. When Grandma was alive, she took joy in spoiling Johnson. He was her only grandson. She did all she could to make Johnson happy, including allowing him to go outside and play with his friends, against her daughter's wish. Johnson felt the loss of his grandma so much, especially when it came to free time to go out and play with his friends.

The older Johnson became, the more he felt the pressure of wanting to be independent as an adolescent. Because of Nicole's restrictions on Johnson, more conflicts developed between Johnson and his mother. When Johnson became a teenager, he fell in love with sports but could not play as much as he wanted. He started asking more questions about his background. He asked his mother why she appeared to be overprotecting him. Nicole replied that it was because he was all she had. In other words, he was very important to her. Nicole told Johnson that her grandma told her that an African proverb said, *"A woman that has only one child owes the ground a debt of one child."* Johnson could not understand his mother's African proverb. He went to Great-Uncle Jo and complained about his mother's overprotection. Johnson told his Great-uncle that, in his opinion, Nicole, his mother, was not doing him any favor. Johnson told Great-Uncle Jo about his mother's African proverb. To Johnson, the proverbs made no sense. Great-Uncle Jo laughed, "Hahahaha," made some sound, "H-u-h-u-h-u," cleared his throat, waited for a minute, and then told Johnson about another African proverb, "Holding a baby to one's chest will not prevent a baby destined to die from dying." After learning from the two African proverbs, it became clear to Johnson that his mother appeared to be struggling with knowing where to draw the line between overprotection and not protecting enough. Johnson had always wanted to be bold, adventurous, and a hero like his ancestors in Africa.

Johnson was now a young adult male, a senior in a high school. He was getting ready to go to college. He was hoping that going to college away from home would give him the opportunity to exercise freedom. Johnson was getting ready to step into a stage of life development that often appears to be faster than other stages of development are. This typical stage is when teenagers leave home for college or start living independently and working. Nicole became conscious of her only son getting ready to leave home. She emphasized to her son the importance of focusing on his studies to succeed in school and life. Johnson recalled the advice of his great-uncle: that a young man is a potential warrior who must be strong, ready to work hard, demand his rights, and prepared to fight and even pay a death sacrifice if necessary to preserve the right and freedom for self, family, and village.

Uncle Jo emphasized that the number one duty of a man is to provide for the family—provide food, shelter, and security. All along, Nicole's intention was to prevent Johnson from knowing what she went through growing up. What her parents and grandparents experienced from white people's racism, prejudice, and discrimination were worse. However, as Johnson became older, he became suspicious of his mother's overprotection. Johnson started feeling that his mother was hiding some information from him. He felt the absence of a father. He asked his mother who his father was and where he was. Nicole was ashamed to tell her son that she was an unwed mother. Nicole told her son that she grew up in a very poor environment. She told Johnson how she became pregnant and how her boyfriend disappeared into thin air. He never had the opportunity to interact and interrelate with his friends as much as he wanted. He wanted to have many friends, but his mother would not allow him to keep friends. His friends started calling him names. This made Johnson very unhappy. In addition to not having real friends, Johnson noticed that white boys and girls discriminated against him and other black teenagers. When the teacher groups white and black students together at school, the white students would refuse to work with black students, indicating that black students were not smart. The teacher would then allow blacks and whites to work separately. By now, Johnson was developing and learning faster about his background. He observed that even teachers showed more interest in white students than black students.

Furthermore, he recalled one occasion in school when a black student was walking behind a white student along a hallway. The white student walked down the hallway, bypassing the principal. The principal said nothing, but when the black student was about to bypass the principal, the principal quickly stopped the black student and said that students were not expected to be walking along that hallway at that time. The principal ordered the black student to his office and gave him after-school detention. The black student was very angry because the white student who did the same thing was not punished.

From conversations with his black friends, Johnson discovered that he was not the only black teenager skeptical about white people's double standards when dealing with black people. He found that majority of black students share the same feelings as he has; many black teenagers tended to feel that white people put them down and call them lazy or unsuitable. In another dimension, Johnson thought many white people appear uneasy when talking about black people, even when they may honestly make an important point about black people. Johnson thought that white people might be conscious of many unjust practices their ancestors legislated and executed on black people. It appeared to Johnson that many white people were always careful not to be seen as racists. Even in churches, Johnson noticed that many white people tended to feel uncomfortable sitting close to black people. He believed that this is the major reason there are black and white churches instead of building common places of worship for everybody (white and black). On another occasion, Johnson had a minor disagreement with a white boy. The white boy told him that he looked like a piece of shit. In an argument that followed, the white boy told Johnson that he was nobody and that Johnson could only be whatever he, as a white boy, said that he was.

Johnson went home and told his mother about his experience. His mother was very sad. She became worried that the very experience she was trying to protect her son from was finally showing its ugly face. Johnson continued to ask more questions about their background, his father, grandfather, and grandmother. He asked his mother to tell him about the history of black people in America. Nicole told him not to worry about discrimination and take his studies very seriously to enable him to become somebody in the future. The mother's advice was not good enough for Johnson.

At this point, Nicole had no more room to hide her experience growing up in America. She was forced to tell her son the truth. Nicole told her son that she does not trust white people but that the situation of black people has improved a lot compared to what it was in the past. Johnson said, "I don't know about trust, but I have many friends among white boys." Nicole gave her son a brief history of how the black people came from Africa to America. She told Johnson that black history in America is a dark secret that she never wanted to expose to him. She explained that the dark history of black people in America was why she did not encourage him to have many friends. She wanted him to be of a positive mind, focus his energy and time on his studies, and to do well in school. Education, she told him, is the key to success in America. From Nicole's story, Johnson concluded that her mother lived with a total disregard for racism, prejudice, and discrimination to be accepted by white people. Johnson decided that there must be a better way and resolved that he must find that better way. He promised himself that he would not live the lifestyle of his mother, that he must make changes. He developed an interest in having more conversations with his Great-Uncle Jo and with his friend Uncle Paul, the retired white man.

With time, Johnson's experiences started affecting his grades in school. He managed to finish his high school and was admitted into a junior college. Johnson was always sad, and he blamed other people for his sad situation. He could not get along with many students and teachers. He was skipping classes and failing his courses. By his second year, his situation resulted in conflicts of interest, and Johnson dropped out of college. He moved back into his mother's home but could not get along with his mother. He moved out of his mother's house and found a low-wage job. Johnson was fired from different jobs. Finally, he secured another position in a warehouse where he worked many hours daily, doing a tedious job that involved heavy lifting. He worked different shifts—morning, afternoon, and sometimes night. At this job, Johnson observed the true color of racism, prejudice, and discrimination. The supervisors, all whites, often assigned blacks to the most challenging jobs.

On the other hand, the white groups were always assigned lighter jobs. Johnson was always tired and was always experiencing body pains. He saw himself in a hole with no easy way out. He had too many questions with, apparently, no answers. One of the questions was why the white people who did lighter jobs were paid more and were receiving promotions. He worked hard for many years in the warehouse, but he noticed that white boys would be employed, and after working for about six months, they would be promoted to be his bosses. On Johnson's off days, he would visit Uncle Jo to socialize with him. Johnson continued to ask questions about culture, race, and ethnicity. He complained about his difficulties and poor condition. Even though Johnson was working hard, he could not pay his bills. Uncle Jo told Johnson that high positions at work were not for black people. Uncle Jo emphasized the importance of education. Uncle Jo said, "Education, education, education is the answer."

One source of joy for Johnson was Uncle Jo's African folklore that Uncle Jo learned from his grandfather when he was alive. The stories were much fun for Johnson. Uncle Jo told Johnson that he took pride in staying close to old relatives, and that helped him learn about the history of about five generations of their ancestors. His grandpa told him about life in Africa and how their ancestors came to America in chains. He told stories about the shipment of their ancestors from the coast of Africa to America. Johnson said that the stories about animals and birds sounded as if animals and birds actually talk over there in Africa. Uncle Jo told Johnson that the folklore stories helped bond children and their parents and grandparents. Uncle Jo's typical folklore story was the story of the tortoise and the animals.

The absence of Johnson's biological father was a major factor in his problem. He had no father figure—somebody to look up to while growing up. He had no role model. His only source of strength and guidance came from his relationship with his mother and Uncle Jo. Then came a devastating trauma—the death of Uncle Jo. Johnson recalled what Uncle Jo said, another African proverb, "If you take away what makes a person beautiful, that person's beauty is gone." Uncle Jo was a source of inspiration and empowerment for Johnson, and when he died, the source of encouragement seemed to die also. Johnson decided that it was time to act on all he had learned from Uncle Jo. He resolved that it was time to look for the Africa that was stripped from him. Johnson decided to believe in himself and in his ability to regain his cultural strength. It was time to look for Africa in Africa.

Uncle Jo's folklore:

The Tortoise and Animals

Once, there was a famine in the land of animals. There was nothing to eat. The tortoise was known for its cunningness in the world of animals. The tortoise went in search of food in a nearby bush. Near a palm tree, the tortoise found a dry palm fruit. Inside the palm fruit was encased a seed (palm kernel). The tortoise was very happy. It smashed the palm fruit in between two stones. The palm kernel ejected out of the case some distance away from the tortoise. The palm kernel fell into a hole. This made the tortoise very angry. The tortoise labored very hard to find this one palm fruit. This was not funny to the tortoise. It jumped into the hole, chasing the palm kernel. Inside the hole was ghost children. These ghost children grabbed the palm kernel that the tortoise was chasing. The children challenged the tortoise to a wrestling match. The tortoise responded that only those who were well fed could participate in a wrestling contest. The children took the tortoise to their home, where there was plenty to eat. After eating, the father of the children gave the tortoise a drum and told the tortoise that the drum would provide food for its family when the turtle beats on the drum. The turtle was very happy, thinking that the food problem was solved once and for all. When the turtle got home, it assembled all the family members and beat the drum. There appeared on the table plenty of food, and all members of the family ate full. Next, the turtle assembled all animals in the village to feed them and show them how wealthy the turtle had become. The turtle then beat the drum, and plenty of food appeared on all the tables in the room. All the animals ate and made merry. The following day, the turtle assembled the family again to eat food. After they were all seated, the turtle beat the drum; but there was no food this time. Instead, there were lots of masquerades with sticks in hand. The masquerades whipped the hell out of the turtle and family. The turtle was very angry, and it then decreed that all animals that enjoyed with them must suffer with them. The turtle then assembled the animals again, but the drum was handed over to one of the animal members this time. The turtle instructed the animal holding the drum to beat the drum when all the animals were seated. After this instruction, the turtle and family members cunningly sneaked out of the house through the back door. The animal with the drum then beat the drum, and masquerades jumped out again with whips and severely tortured the animals.

Uncle Jo told Johnson that the story taught the turtle responsibility, meaning that when one has an opportunity, one does not have to misuse it.

Another source of joy. Growing up, Johnson loved watching cowboy movies, especially American icons like John Wayne, Clinton Eastwood,

Kirk Douglas, and many more. Johnson watched cowboys knock themselves down into submission, and after each fight, the man standing up helped the one down get up. He remembered watching some cowboys walk to the same table after fighting and drink whiskey together. He loved cowboys. This memory made Johnson feel that Americans do not internalize anger. He remembered Uncle Paul saying that Americans are very generous; they are also a people who can always stop those who make their "mules" mad. Johnson loved America being always courageous and very strong. Because Johnson trusted the wisdom of his old friend Uncle Paul, he believed him. Johnson concluded that for him to become a great American, he must give up all anger and put all his energy into taking advantage of the numerous opportunities that America offered him concerning education, job opportunities, liberty, and freedom unparalleled anywhere in the world. But first, Johnson must travel to Africa and regain his originality. He believed he could get along easily with black boys and white boys when he brought closure to the hole in his heart. To Johnson, his originality would help him overcome his anger and create equality with people of other cultural backgrounds. He realized that he could not interrelate positively with others with anger in his heart. Johnson made a conscious decision to externalize his problems. He gave names to his problem situations. For example, he called racism Humpty. When Johnson encountered a racist situation, he would smile and call it by its name. "Humpty, you know that I deserve happiness, and I never allow any situation or environment to take away my desire." Johnson believed that if racism saw Africa in him, racism would run away and disappear forever. He said that when he comes back from Africa, he will be a different person, color-blind, and with a high self-esteem. He would be able to interrelate with other boys (black and white) confidently and compete equally in all works of life.

CHAPTER 2

Who Am I

A time came when Johnson decided that he must stop complaining about conflicts of interests and get something straight—be able to define who he is as an African American. To add to the knowledge from his mother and Great-Uncle Jo, Johnson asked Uncle Paul to help him reason why he was finding problems defining himself, getting along with people (blacks and whites), and concentrating on things he wanted to achieve. Uncle Paul told Johnson that he might not be alone among his peers. He told Johnson that the majority of black teenagers growing up seemed to have something in common, and that is growing up accepting negative stereotypes stigmatized to them by the white majority. This situation appeared to place a frustrating pressure on black teenagers like him, making it difficult for him to talk about racism, prejudice, and discrimination.

In Uncle Paul's opinion, many black teenagers like Johnson seemed to accept a negative evaluation from many white people even though Johnson disagreed with negative labeling not to be seen as making excuses to explain his failures. For black teenagers who behaved like Johnson's parents did, instead of being who they are, they seemed to prefer working toward pleasing white people to be accepted by them. According to Johnson, this was exactly what his mother was doing.

Johnson felt that expressing any feeling different from his mother's feeling (lifestyle) was interpreted as conflicting with the norm established by the white majority. After talking with Johnson, Uncle Paul said that Johnson's self-concept seemed to refer to his beliefs, desires, values, and attributes with which Johnson can be defined. In his opinion, the key parts of Johnson's self-concept included his wanting to be a warrior like his ancestors and his desire to regain the African cultural strength that was stripped off his ancestors. In answering questions from Johnson, Uncle Paul told Johnson that because blacks like him were not allowed by whites of the slave era to create a construct of their own environment, they could not relate to the society around them based on their interpretation of the world around them. Johnson agreed that Uncle Paul's observation was one of the causes of his anger when he related to white people. It made him feel like white people pushed him around. Johnson recalled that according to Uncle Paul, many black people could not achieve normal human development because the white man's legislation and policies did not allow their genes to achieve healthy interaction with their day-to-day experience.

Consequently, as an African American, Johnson could not achieve optimum productivity because he tended to wait for approval or disapproval of his behaviors from white people. Johnson said to himself that the white man's type of slavery yielded dividends for them in the short run by cheap labor but failed in the long run when slavery could not provide optimum productivity. Johnson opined that the more blacks like him lived a black-white American lifestyle, the more America lost valuable resources. This could be estimated to be billions or trillions of dollars, as evidenced by the huge number of black teenagers like him who are unable to find and maintain jobs many more who are in jail, not counting teenagers who are mentally incapacitated. Johnson believed that the expectation of blacks like him to perform at optimum level required him to behave as an original African American and not as a black-white American. He saw the term *black American* as African American devoid of African roots. Johnson believed that European Americans function at an advantage because they have European roots in them, and so should he, as African Americans have African roots in them.

Dr. Paul said to Johnson, "I really think you need psychotherapy treatment. I know that you might not understand what I am talking about, so let us discuss what I say in a dialogue."

> Johnson: What is psychotherapy?
> Dr. Paul: A form of treatment that can help you learn to perceive your problem differently and change from negative to positive behavior.
> Johnson: I like that. Who can help me to change?
> Dr. Paul: Psychiatrists, psychologists, or other professionally trained mental health therapists.
> Johnson: Can you recommend me to them?
> Dr. Paul: Yes, I can, but you have to trust them and be ready to tell the story about your negative life experiences accurately, all you can remember.
> Johnson: Uncle Paul, I am ready to do anything to recover my self-concept and be a happy person.
> Dr. Paul: But I must warn you, change does not come easily.
> Johnson: Uncle Paul, you do not understand. My life is like hell on earth. I will do anything to come out of my hell and live a normal life. Will they prescribe medication for me?
> Dr. Paul: I don't think you will need medication in

your situation. However, they will do an assessment of your problems and develop a treatment plan for your treatment objectives. Some professionals call this type of treatment a talking cure.

Johnson: Do you mean they will be advising me on how to behave well?

Dr. Paul: It is not just talking to you. Their talk is clinical if you know what I mean.

Johnson: I am afraid I do not know what you mean.

Dr. Paul: I think you know that I am a registered psychologist, but you also know that I am now retired. I will make an appointment for you to see a mental health professional—a psychiatrist, a psychologist, or a professionally trained therapist.

Johnson: Did I hear you say *mental health*?

Dr. Paul: Yes, your problem is a mental health issue.

Johnson: Uncle Paul, I am not crazy. I am only not happy, and that makes me angry very often. I can tell you this. I do not believe that a white man was talking to me about the injustice and racism that other white people purposely perpetuated on my ancestors, parents, and myself will help me change to become better. Actually, that may help to increase my anger because I may not trust them.

Dr. Paul: Johnson, you do not understand. These professionals are specially trained and licensed to offer such services. They have been able to help people that have worse a problem than yours.

Johnson: Can the psychiatrist be able to undo my past negative history?

Dr. Paul: If your question asks for a guarantee, the
answer is no. But they will work with you to help
you to be able to challenge yourself to change
into a new life course. I believe that you can do it.
Psychotherapy has been able to help people with
the worst mental health problems.
Johnson: Uncle Paul, I will think about it and give you
my answer tomorrow.

The following day, Johnson went to Uncle Paul and told him that he was grateful for his concern about his (Johnson's) problems. "I believe that your treatment may work for me, but that might take longer. I also have a concern about possible relapses. However, I heard a voice tell me in a dream a long time ago that I can never be stable until I return to Africa and recover my originality." Johnson seemed to lack trust, which is important in counseling therapy. Johnson felt strongly about his dream. He said that he also wanted to go to Africa for some other personal reasons. "I must go to Africa to recover my African roots," Johnson said that he believed that his problem was caused by the loss of Africa in him. He thought that he needed to regain his cultural roots and that when he came back from Africa, he would be perfectly stable.

Johnson believed that he did not need to be a white man to achieve the same things or better than a white man does. He argued that he did not need to borrow white roots and pretend to be a white man. Doing that would place him at a disadvantage. In Johnson's opinion, that was exactly what his mother and her parents did in the past, and all they got was government welfare. He recognized poverty as one of the ills of slavery. He was born into poverty, but he promised himself that he must do all he could to recover his African cultural values. He said to himself that he must be responsible for his actions in doing this.

Johnson believed that his travel to Africa was his own form of treatment that would enable him to move himself out of poverty. For Johnson, the biggest community issue of goodness is family. He perceived family as a unit of society. However, Johnson was not thinking of relating to total African culture; instead, he desired to recover his African cultural background on which to adjust to European American culture. He thought that this would put him into a proper American melting pot. Johnson felt that he was being viewed through others' cultural forms of reference. He saw himself as a manipulated black person and different from who he actually is—an African American. According to his old friend Uncle Paul, only African Americans were forced to give up all their cultural values to become Americans.

In contrast, other people from other cultural backgrounds built their American citizenship on some previous cultural foundation. In his opinion, he felt that this made him be whatever the white people wanted him to be. As an African American, Johnson had to borrow everything of value: language, fashion, food, family structure, and so on. Johnson felt that the European culture expected him to master what his parents learned. To him, that would mean mastering what was unfittingly imposed on his parents. Johnson believed that if he regains his African cultural roots, then he can smoothly adjust to whatever he learns to fit into his original African culture. This process would enable him to transform into a stable African American.

Johnson's Great-Uncle Jo told him that the white people destroyed what they could not recreate by stripping cultural values off African Americans. Johnson learned that the early African Americans who arrived in America as slaves were angry, disrespected, and afraid. His ancestors transferred this culture of fear, disrespect, and anger to their children. Therefore, Johnson was not surprised about his constant anger and conflict in dealing with people, especially people of different cultural backgrounds. With all the above experiences, Johnson perceived a sense of urgency to act and make a change for better welfare in his life. Nicole, Johnson's mother, perceived the same problem long ago but was afraid to talk about the long-needed change. For Johnson, he felt that the warrior genes of his ancestors were in him, and he resolved that he must act and find the Africa missing in him. His mother and her parents did not act because they were chasing whiteness to be accepted in society. His parents did not know that chasing whiteness was like chasing their own shadows.

Johnson said that his parents were supposed to be honest with themselves and be who they were. For Johnson, therein lies his strength, confidence, stability, wholeness, and true self-concept. They were made to see black as ugly. In contrast, Johnson believed that black is a color just as white is. He argued that if black was not beautiful, why do many white people dress in black and choose to own and drive black cars? Some white people even answer to the name *black*. Johnson believed that white people chose black because they liked it as a color, just as some black people dressed in white and chose to drive in white cars. After all, is equally beautiful. Unfortunately, Nicole and her parents were contented with what the white people gave to them. They were afraid to live their beliefs. To Johnson, only when he believes in himself will he be able to contribute and participate successfully in this ever-changing world. Johnson wanted to defeat fear. He said that he was ready to make mistakes and learn from his mistakes.

He observed that his mother and her family and families like them did not appear to understand the true urgency for change. They wanted to change for better lives, but their desire to change was influenced by wanting to be seen as nice people. But they missed the point that the need for change has nothing to do with nicety and has everything to do with being whole and stable. Therein lies their ability to forge ahead without being afraid of failing, the ability to compete with people from other cultural groups, and also the ability to bargain competently in any situation. Johnson learned from Dr. Paul that being competent promotes creativity and success, be it in education, business, or other aspects of life. He said that his mother and her family's settling for less had consequences, including some of his problems growing up. He argued that his mother and family continued to hope that the white people would do their thinking and change of behavior for them. The result was an accumulation of lost resources. This helped create in him and, most likely, other peers' frustration, teenage pregnancy, school dropout problems, poverty, anger, and various psychological disorders. For Johnson, the above experiences called for a desire to find his African cultural strength and the ability to act and achieve the long-needed positive change. On one occasion, he asked Dr. Paul if he had any idea why the Africans sold his descendants into slavery. Dr. Paul told Johnson that slavery reduced his ancestors to a condition unworthy of human beings.

Still, whatever were the intentions of the Africans who sold them and the white people who bought them as slaves, sometimes, things happen for a purpose. Dr. Paul asked Johnson if he goes to church. Johnson said that he used to go with his mother but not anymore since he started living by himself. However, Dr. Paul told Johnson the story of a man called Joseph in the Bible. Joseph's brothers sold him to Egyptian traders to live the rest of his life as a slave. While in Egypt, Joseph did not forget his core value: that he was a Jew who believed and trusted his god. He built his lifestyle in Egypt on his core cultural value. The result was that instead of living as a slave, he rose to the rank of prime minister in the king's palace. Dr. Paul said that the point he was making was that Joseph could not have become a prime minister if he was not sold into slavery. Johnson trusted the wisdom of Dr. Paul and started thinking that it could be that his ancestors were sold to America to take advantage of the opportunities in America and become "kings" and "queens." This thought process made Johnson hopeful. But first, like Joseph, he must regain the cultural values of his ancestors, take advantage of the opportunities in America, and build his African American status on his original African roots.

CHAPTER 3

The Absence of Ethnicity and Culture

"The sacred rights of mankind are not to be rummaged for, among old parchments, or musty records. They are written, as with a sun beam in the whole volume of human nature, by the hand of the divinity itself; and can never be erased or obscured by mortal power."

–Alexander Hamilton, 1775

Johnson learned that ethnicity eincludes a group of people with ethnic affiliation—people with distinguished customs, characteristics, language, common history, rituals, common beliefs, and patterns of behavior. These attributes, Johnson learned, constitute the contents of a people's ethnic culture. For a people, this cultural ethnicity forms a foundation of sacred values, which the people reserve the right to adjust and develop as they live. In his opinion, stripping culture off African American ancestors means making them start all over to learn and build a new culture based on other people's values. But Johnson never heard of any people starting cultural development from scratch. Uncle Jo said that for Johnson, as an African American, to start all over would require him to start on a clean slate with no beliefs, no value system, no family structure or experience of any kind. He has to give up his roots and relationships with his original cultural history. In Africa, in particular, such behavior is taboo. The reason is that the people's culture is a sacred guide given to the people or handed down to the African ancestors by their creator. Uncle Jo told Johnson that to start all over means destroying the blueprint of who he is. For Johnson, when his people's blueprint is lost, any definition or description of him is guesswork. And if he starts by guessing who he is, then every aspect of his life loses original value. Uncle Jo emphasized that any human being cannot forge a people's culture because the sacred beliefs of Africans evolved from humans who went before them.

According to Uncle Jo, the sacredness of African culture defines African American ancestors as people of an ethnic group who believe in working hard to provide for themselves, a people known for their strong sense of family love. Johnson loved the idea that in Africa, depending on other people for daily living is a cultural shame and, in fact, a taboo. This belief is so sacred, strong, and real that it is enshrined in the worship of their god above, whom they depend upon to bless them with abundance during harvests and who has never disappointed them. Johnson learned that an ethnic African is honest, hardworking, and family-oriented. According to Uncle Jo, a community that has honest, hardworking families is very likely to succeed because the members of those families would look at public issues with the community in mind. This belief includes the expected responsibility of each member's actions, and consequences for a member deemed lazy. Jo observed that African ancestors always worked with ethnic African families in mind. They subscribed to activities that were suitable for group members. Similarly, they achieved more when they worked with suitable plans for their groups, and achieved less when they were pressured to adopt plans that required specific groups.

Because of the sacredness of culture, Johnson believed that he deserved the right to use his cultural background as a foundation on which to adopt a more widespread culture and then adjust to a balance. In his opinion, adjusting to a more popular gestalt culture is respectful to his minority culture, while replacing his cultural background is disrespectful to his minority culture. Replacing culture means creating different beliefs, rights, and values entirely new to the minority. Johnson learned that no human has the right to force this change on other humans, and when this happens, the minorities tend to continue to behave dissatisfied in all works of their lives. The result is a tendency for conflicts, even when there is no need or reason for disagreement. Often, disagreements on current issues can be based on past dissatisfied issues that may not have any bearing on the current issues. It could become almost impossible for the majority group to satisfy the minority group in some situations. Johnson found in his neighborhood that some unnecessary conflicts were interpreted as resulting from unintended consequences of old rules passed by the majority culture and forced on the minority culture. Uncle Jo said that in America, the white government used to deny poor black single parents (mothers) some government assistance if the African American woman was living with a man in the house. This made the man leave the house on days that a government official would be going to check whether a man lives with the applicant for government benefits. This practice encouraged the black man in the house to stay away from home. This apparently promoted single parenthood in society, especially in the African American community. However, Uncle Jo explained to Johnson that the white government was conducting the check for the man in the family to make him accept the responsibility of working to provide for his family. Uncle Jo argued along with Johnson that the government stripped away black men's family responsibility when they stripped away their culture.

Consequently, racist government policies helped make many black men learn irresponsibility in their families. After stripping away the naturally black African values to manipulate the black man into free labor, the government then came back to recreate what they destroyed. Johnson had the experience of a single-parenthood family because his mother was unwed and born into poverty. After hundreds of years since the African American roots were destroyed, the white government has been trying without success to recreate what it stripped away. In Johnson's opinion, the white government's policies destroyed the Africa inside those fathers who were running away from their family responsibilities and then destroyed the Africa inside Johnson. This deficiency, according to Johnson, is responsible for his excessive anger, school dropout problems, anxiety, depression, and other psychological problems. From his experience, Johnson concluded that the absence of Africa in him caused him to behave strangely. As a result, his school teacher, who expected him to act in a certain responsible manner, and his work supervisor, who expected him to stay away from conflicts, looked the Africa in Johnson that was stripped away. Uncle Jo compared the expectations of Johnson's teacher and his supervisor at work to an African proverb, "Caregiver destroyed the toy with which a baby was playing and kept asking the baby to find the toy." This insinuates that the caregiver does not know where the toy is. The above expectations seem to be pointing in the same direction that America is looking for Africa in Johnson. By America, Johnson included African Americans, white Americans, and others of other cultural origins.

Johnson's friend Uncle Paul felt that diversity has helped America grow strong. However, he also felt that America still needs more respect for cultural differences and more appreciation for values that exist in different cultures. He regretted that minority cultural groups still have a long way to achieve equal opportunity because economic opportunities in America still continue to favor people from majority cultural groups more than they favor people from minority cultures. Uncle Paul argued that time would tell whether it was worth it to exclude the culture and ethnicity of African Americans in the building of American social society. Johnson asked the following question to his friend, "Uncle Paul, in your opinion, what did loss of ethnicity do to the upbringing of a black child?" Uncle Paul replied, "Loss of love, low self-esteem, low self-concept, weak bargaining and competitive power, and lack of motivation to perform." Johnson was concerned that he suffered all the above emotional problems. For Johnson, the effects of whiteness became the epitome of his character. His character was dominated by his tendency to be angry. He was often angry because he found that the white ethnicity was always positioned to dictate how he would behave or respond instead of being allowed to figure out issues or changes into African American ethnicity to work for him.

Uncle Jo told Johnson that he needed to be informed of some of the fallacies of the slave masters: the idea that the African American ancestors never had a community until they came to America and that they came to America and quickly replaced their love for their ancestors with love for their new experience of group formation. Uncle Jo lamented and said that these slave masters were very disrespectful and, in fact, very insulting to the African American ancestors, whose families were kings, chiefs, cabinet members, and warriors. Uncle Jo added that the ancestors were great people. They were people from a great civilization with a stable government in West Africa, from where the majority of black ancestors came. Johnson asked Uncle Jo why the white people did not strip off their own culture so that everybody would start all over at the same time. Uncle Jo replied by saying that the white people felt that everything white was superior and everything about blacks was inferior. The practice was that only black people who passed the whiteness test were seen as whites or admitted into the society. Most of these black-white people were described as group conscious. But in Johnson's opinion, an African American who falls into this category can only pretend to be white. Johnson figured, however, that cultural roots could not be replaced with any type of consciousness to be optimally operational. gAccording to Johnson's friend Uncle Paul, one thing is certain for Johnson to become a solid American, he must first be an African. He learned that he would lack the receptors for the many opportunities in America without that base. Uncle Paul added that because some black people have continued to complain about unfair treatment, and rightly so, however, those black people are not completely free. He observed that many black people had achieved remarkable social/economic success. However, the tradition of the majority in society still tends to regard black Americans as a racial group instead of a cultural group.

Consequently, this stigma has continued to adversely result in psychological problems for African Americans. Uncle Paul, on another note, expressed his disappointment for the limited attention that scholars show to ethnicity and social factors in health studies on people of African ancestry. This lack of adequate information makes health professionals unable to easily diagnose and treat Johnson's behavioral problems.

CHAPTER 4

The Melting Pot

As Johnson understood, all immigrants in America came with their different cultures and ethnicities from other countries. Johnson learned that each group of immigrants was progressive in their way of life and wanted to maintain their lifestyle. However, the immigrants from England were among the first people to arrive in America. They were also the highest in number at the time. Because the English immigrants already knew what democracy was, they believed they deserved the right to determine how the immigrants should be administered based on their number in society. Uncle Paul explained to Johnson what civilized people call democracy: government of the people, by the people, for the people. Johnson waited for a minute and remembered Uncle Paul saying that democracy is also majority rule and minority right. Uncle Paul said yes, it is true. Johnson then argued, "How then did the European Americans benefit both ways? They took charge of the government and beat the hell out of my ancestors. They did not protect the interests of the minority." Uncle Paul replied, "Johnson, you know that sometimes stuff happens."

"What is *stuff*?" Johnson asked.

"You may call it injustice or racism, and added that democracy does not guarantee justice, only the process of justice through the court of law, and if one does not have the resources with which to fight for one's rights, one may not have any right or denied rights."

Johnson concluded, "I think that was exactly what happened to my ancestors and from my ancestors to me." The English immigrants made a conscious decision that because they were more in number, they deserved the right to impose their culture on other minority cultures. Johnson felt that it must have been easy for people from European countries to adapt to the Anglo-Saxon ethnicity. Still, it must have been difficult for people from minority countries like Africa to make a quick ethnic change to the Western way of life. As a result, his ancestors were subjected to a very difficult change in the situation because, according to Uncle Paul, a people's culture is usually infused into the lifestyle of the people.

Rightly so, according to the democratic rule, the Europeans that were more in number had to impose their culture on the minorities. Johnson's concern was that the slave masters made no effort to protect the interests of the minorities, like his ancestors, who were forced to give up their values to be accepted into the majority group. In Johnson's opinion, the English immigrants arrogated themselves to the position of superiority and relegated immigrants from minority countries to an inferior position. The majority ethnicity then had to determine who was good enough to be admitted or assimilated into the status of whiteness. Johnson said that the issue of whiteness at this time became a yardstick with which an individual's acceptability in society was measured. If one were accepted or described as white, one would enjoy a superior status in society. This meant that the white person would have the privilege of being respected in society. The person would qualify for a good-paying job even if another applicant from the minority group appeared to be more qualified. Because the power that manipulated the central ethnicity had total control over who would be assimilated, a group that was assimilated got good-paying jobs and qualified for a high standard of living. This resulted in people from minority cultures accepting low-paying jobs, which led to a low standard of living. This inequality situation was worst for people like Johnson and his family, whose background was rooted in African origin. Invariably, the Europeans thought of what they would gain without considering to what the minorities would lose (especially the African Americans, whose culture was completely stripped).

ePeople like Johnson did not only get low-paying jobs, but they also had to suffer discrimination in the workplace. Johnson was told that the African Americans and the American Indians were perceived as people that were not assimilable into the society. Worse still, some white people feel that assimilating dark-skinned African Americans would threaten the purity of white-skinned people. Johnson learned that this mindset existed because some white people intended to develop an ethnocentric society that would create an ideological gestalt that would be identified with whiteness. Johnson figured that because the English people were among the first immigrants to arrive in America and because they were more in number than other early immigrants, they saw an opportunity to take control of the affairs of the society and took it. They followed their capture of authority to expect others to see things their way. As it were, the English Europeans apparently dictated how much identity outside Anglo-Saxon culture would be allowed in a society dominated by Western culture. Johnson was told that all other minority groups except African Americans came to the melting pot with their cultures infused in them. It was, therefore, virtually impossible for any cultural group not to leave a trace of their heritage in the melting pot. But the African Americans came into the melting pot empty-handed because the white masters used force to strip African culture away from African American ancestors. However, the melting pot united members from different ethnic groups into one common ethnicity. The problem for people like Johnson was that they were not allowed to contribute anything of their culture to the pot. According to Johnson, his ancestors were forced into coming to borrow from others instead of coming to mix with others in the pot as designed by the Founding Fathers. As a result, my ancestors lost their sense of contact with their origin, and had since then continued to be a problem for them and their descendants. All other attendants at the pot came with their own group's culture infused in them, while the African ancestors lost their group's culture and suffered all sorts of inhuman punishments. Punishment included severe flogging, biting, and separation from biological family, all for them to accept what and who the slave masters wanted them to be. In Johnson's opinion, the African American ancestors going through the pot did tremendous damage to them and their descendants. They were forced to accept varying degrees of others' cultures that melted out, with nothing melting from them into other members in the pot.

For Johnson, this was the foundation of generations of injustice, discrimination, racism, school dropouts, low self-esteem, low self-concept, inability to compete squarely, teenage pregnancy, anger, frustration, poverty, and many more ills. His ancestors came into the pot with a cultural hole in them. After looking at the plight of people of African American descent like him, Johnson was left with nothing but questions. Why do people from other ethnic backgrounds, like the Asians and the European Americans, stay in school while people from an African background, like him, drop out of school? Why do they exercise patience and learn the trade and work skills to enable them to find and keep jobs, and people like him could not? Why does a higher proportion of teenagers of his own descent, more than that of other cultural groups' teenagers, languish in jail? Why do many sisters of his descent have many children out of wedlock, with the fathers of the children nowhere to be found? Of all these questions, Johnson could only come up with one answer, and it is that the people of his cultural descent lost their original cultural background. He remembered again what he learned—that the strains of people's culture are naturally infused into the lifestyle of the people. Johnson learned that the tenets of a people's culture put the people in a group identified with a unifying relationship. This relationship character dictates how people think, feel, and communicate. These are wholeness qualities that help structure the people into a unique group within the overall big American group in the society. Of course, the big American group has many other similar subgroups. But the unique qualities help each subgroup to maintain a balance in the society as the members of each subgroup go through changes. The group's maintained balance enables the members to create their own goals as they live interdependently in society. It became clear to Johnson that when the culture of his people was stripped away, this natural procedure of the group process was also stripped away, making it very difficult for him to be stable and successful. Johnson remembered one of his many dialogues with his Uncle Jo.

It went like this:

Uncle Jo: Johnson, I think you know that the crop seed beans absorb much water when cooked. [I am talking about the activities in a typical, day-to-day life functioning in a typical African village.]

Johnson: Yes, I do.

Uncle Jo: Nobody plans to cook beans without having some water of their own.

Johnson: And why is it so, Uncle Jo?

Uncle Jo: It is because you will never have enough water for cooking the beans. The tendency is that you

would end up burning your beans because you will
never be able to borrow all the water you will need.

In this dialogue, Uncle Jo was making clear to Johnson the importance of one's own unique cultural (ethnic) background on which to build one's new culture. It was not a matter of whether one would have it. Uncle Jo said that it is a part of the whole human being. According to Uncle Jo, a human being who lacks this essential will continue lacking it all through life, and the effects of the deficiency are huge. Uncle Jo said that the lack of wholeness in an individual affects the proper growth and development of the person. Jo said that the original culture-deficient individual will always find difficulty maintaining a stable lifestyle, even after achieving academic and financial success. For Johnson, the consolation is the freedom/liberty that the American Constitution provided to all citizens and his desire and willingness to change his situation. Johnson believed that his unfortunate situation would completely change when he found Africa. This means reactivating the strains of his original African culture. There is no substitute for this original part of Johnson's self. Johnson's dialogues with his Great-Uncle Jo helped him understand the importance of his originality.

Johnson asked his old friend Uncle Paul why his family and others like them did not speak up for their freedom and justice. Uncle Paul told him, "Son, the answer is simple—fear." Paul told Johnson that his ancestors did not speak up because they did not want to be seen as bad people by the slave masters. "Instead, your ancestors chose to conform to social pressures. Your ancestors decided against their wish to live and continued to look up to the white masters for approval for virtually all their life activities. Actually, this perpetuated a feeling of emptiness in the lives of the majority of your ancestor."

In contrast, Uncle Paul said he has much praise and thanks for people like Dr. Martin Luther King Jr. for speaking up and doing the right thing for America. He paid the ultimate price for which America will forever thank him for not giving up freedom and liberty as an American. Uncle Paul stated that some slave masters saw the assimilation of African Americans as a favor that should make them happy and help them forget whatever they lost in their culture and ethnicity, even with racism, prejudice, and discrimination in place. Johnson learned from Uncle Jo that his ethnicity is his link to his ancestors, and without this link, Johnson has no claim to membership of his ancestral origin. Johnson felt that the civil unrest of the 1960s among African Americans who were sick and tired of being made second-class citizens continued the opposition that started at the Mediterranean coast in Africa, where slaves were shipped. He tried to relate his people's opposition to the social pressures he was subjected to. Johnson did not find any sense in the white masters' beliefs that assimilating Europeans from countries with similar beliefs and values would be similar to assimilating people from countries on a different continent. For example, Africa has different beliefs, rituals, languages, and other values. To Johnson, the white masters' extension of whiteness to his ancestors did not solve many problems because, according to Uncle Jo, the African ancestors valued their culture as their lives.

To Johnson, America is a place where immigrants or ethnic groups come and take advantage of opportunities not found in their homeland, develop themselves, and contribute to the building of their new homeland. However, Johnson felt that he could not take advantage of those opportunities because he was stripped of his cultural strength and reduced to a second-class citizen. Johnson said that he could not contribute much to nation-building as long as he remained in his present class. Living in his present class is like being in prison in an egocentric society of slave masters.

Johnson saw himself as a human being reduced to a piece of property by the white masters using their suppressive rules and regulations. This sense of identity made Johnson feel like starting his immigration journey all over, going back to his origin to become original. He started thinking of going back to Africa—his roots—bonding himself with the African soil and then making a conscious decision for a "second" coming to America. Johnson intended to put an end to what his ancestors went through, living by the social pressures imposed on them, and from them to himself. Johnson resolved that he must deal with his problems to avoid transferring them to his children. In his opinion, this would help to make sense of any economic or educational success. He must reverse his identity from being a white African American to being African American. Johnson said to himself that he must first be an African before being an American, a process similar to other immigrants who became American citizens. By African, Johnson meant the concept of the original African ancestors who arrived in America as their own masters, not as slaves. He learned that those Africans knew and cherished the importance of education. He learned that education started in Africa and from Africa to the rest of the world, including America. He learned about the origin of alphabets and writing during the Egyptian civilization and about the Sankore University in Timbuktu. Johnson learned that the Sankore University was a scientific center of learning that operated during a period that corresponded with the European medieval and Renaissance eras. Johnson admired the intelligence of his African ancestors' original family structure. Johnson was talking of his ancestors who took care of his family as their responsibility, the African ancestors who were proud of their self-concepts, and who saw handouts as disrespectful to their pride. This typical ancestor was color-blind and never needed anybody to educate them on the importance of education, family values, school dropout problem, and other similar problems.

Johnson was asking questions as to why the white ethnic majority designed the society to demand that the members of the minority do more to prove competence before achieving equal opportunity in occupations and living standards. He felt that the effects of the slave-era government policies resulted intentionally or unintentionally in perpetual poverty for people like him and his family. For Johnson, a feeling of vacuum inside him has a continuum effect on his life. This real feeling has been in his family for generations. In Johnson's opinion, no amount of economic or educational success could fill the empty space in him. He remembered his uncle Jo telling him that a person of second-class citizenship never held prominent positions. Second-class citizens are always used for duties. They do the job, and the first-class citizens get the benefits. For Johnson, the melting pot created a feeling of second-class citizenship for his ancestors and continues to be an unreachable image like chasing his own shadow. He found that he must stop waiting for the white master to solve his problems. He is the one that must solve his own problem. He must find the Africa that is missing in him and be able to take advantage of the numerous advantages in America.

CHAPTER 5

Johnson and His Peers

Johnson was the only child of his mother. He did not know who his father was or what he looked like. He grew up lacking brothers or sisters to play within the home. This background made Johnson hurry to grow up fast, make friends, and socialize with his friends. Unfortunately, Johnson's mother had a different plan for her son. Nicoles planned to prevent Johnson from knowing the painful past of African Americans. Her intention was to help Johnson stay positive and be able to put all his energies into developing himself, doing well in school, and growing up to be successful. The result here was conflict between Johnson and his mother. Johnson sought relief from his uncle Jo; he became more attached and bonded to Uncle Jo. His uncle had the greatest influence on his life. Johnson has always wanted to be a courageous young man. From the day Uncle Jo told him that his ancestors were warriors, Johnson said to himself, "Now I know why I'm always angry when the white folks seem to dictate how to live my life." He started working hard toward developing his love for a courageous lifestyle. He wanted to be tough, hardworking, and a person of influence in life. Unfortunately, Johnson's wish did not relate well with how he felt treated in society, in school, and among his peers. Mostly white boys who he felt looked down on him. The result was Johnson being involved in conflicts in his relationships.

Relationship with African American teenagers. Johnson's mother expected him to identify himself more with fellow black boys, but it was not completely the case. Johnson saw his fellow black peers as too subservient to white teenagers. In contrast, Johnson saw himself wanting to behave like white boys. Sometimes Johnson felt superior to white teenagers because he believed that warrior ancestry was in his genes. Johnson measured superiority by how strong and courageous one is. His ambition of being first among his equals made him feel like a white boy among his fellow black peers. He hated the attitude of accepting social pressures from white people to be accepted by them. Johnson sometimes feels misplaced when he is in the company of fellow black brothers. On one occasion, a friend of his told him, "Johnson, you don't know what it means to be a black boy in America." In the boy's opinion, it meant accepting second-class status. For Johnson, this meant low self-concept and low self-esteem. Johnson told his black brothers that they perceived being African American backward. He said that he was aware that the American society was designed for him as a black boy to be poor. But the fact remains that he was thinking of the ability of the original African American who came into America as his own master. He was talking about doing whatever it takes to transform himself into the status and capability of his original ancestors. Johnson told his black brothers what he learned from his friend Dr. Paul—that, in fact, the rest of the world, including America, learned from the civilization in Africa. Dr. Paul talked about the knowledge from the Egyptian civilization and the intellectualism at the Sankore University in Timbuktu in Africa. From what he learned from Uncle Paul, Johnson expressed his belief that education is not a white thing, and if anything, it is a black thing, given his understanding of the origin of learning. Johnson told his black brothers that he was beginning to feel that what he needed was not in the hands of white people. "No," he said, "what I need is Africa that was lost in America." He said that when he finds Africa, he will be able to solve his school dropout problem, excessive frustration and anger, and inability to relate with fellow blacks and whites at school and in the workplace. Johnson said to his black brothers, "I don't know about you, but for me, I must do whatever it takes to find my lost ethnicity." Johnson said that he knew some people who were born poor but who achieved great success. Then Johnson asked, "If some were born poor and could achieve success, why can't other poor people like me achieve the same or more success?" This does not mean that Johnson thought that such achievement would be easy in any way. To Johnson, the loss of Africa in him distorted his ability to fully use his natural strength for thinking and feeling and his ability to behave intentionally. It became clear to Johnson that he could not achieve his best in life without reversing his cultural deficiency. He must go back to Africa and regain originality and stability. With time, this thought about his loss translated into Johnson believing it was a fact and influenced his thought process and behavior. His belief about his loss made him blame others for his failure to succeed. However, Johnson said to himself, "There is a solution." He believed that he had the liberty and freedom to empower himself by following his insight to regain his natural strength embedded in the culture of his ancestors. His belief repeatedly drummed the urgency for change from his mind into his body. The result was a final decision to travel to Papa's land in Africa. Johnson learned that over 90% of all African Americans came from the coast of West Africa. The countries would primarily include Senegal, Gambia, Ivory Coast, Ghana, Cameroon, and Nigeria. Now that Johnson had narrowed down the possible area of origin of his ancestors, Johnson worked harder, seeking information from the embassies of West African countries in America to locate the village of his ancestors. Finally, he discovered the Ozuzumba village as the village of his ancestors.

Johnson made some studies and asked questions about the people of Ozuzumba. The information and answers that Johnson collected appeared to match the values that he learned from Uncle Jo. Johnson said to himself, "So far, so good." He did not discuss his lack of originality problem with his black brothers. He withheld his psychological problem within himself. Of course, internalizing negative emotions always resulted in anger and conflicts with his peers and people in authority. Johnson preferred to behave how he should, instead of accepting second-class status to be accepted in society. He felt that pretending to be what society wanted him to be meant more psychological pain for him.

Relationships with white teenagers. Johnson tended to identify with white teenagers because he admired their expression of high self-concept. However, Johnson had a problem with them because he found that many white teenagers did not want to accept him as equal. In Johnson's opinion, the white teenagers who did not appear comfortable accepting him as equal seemed to be behaving in the way they learned from some white parents. This was not very surprising to Johnson because his mother, Nicole, suffered the same experience growing up. Johnson enjoyed a good relationship with some white boys and saw those who did not respect him as ignorant. The ignorant white kids were ready to be friendly with Johnson as long as he was ready to recognize them as superiors.

Johnson would not accept second-class status and often would not say a word about it. Instead, he internalized the pain of being rejected. So, Johnson had a problem relating with black peers, and he also could not get along comfortably with many white teenagers. In high school, Johnson found himself in trouble every week. This caused him to be suspended many times in school. When Johnson started working in a warehouse, his conflict became worse. In the workplace, Johnson experienced racism, discrimination, and prejudice. This made him feel like hating white people. However, Johnson found out quickly that hating white people would not do him any good, as Johnson was fired from different jobs where the supervisors were all whites. He struggled in his relationships with his peers in school and at work and with respecting people in authority, who were often people of white ethnicity.

Johnson decided to do something that would enable him to turn things in his favor and take advantage of the opportunities in America. Johnson decided to think over the wise words of Uncle Jo. Johnson learned that sometimes the door to one's destiny requires a huge sacrifice before it opens. Johnson started thinking smart that his ancestors' sufferings were like the ultimate prize that they paid to give him and the people of his ancestry the chance to take advantage of the opportunities open to them in America—opportunities not available to any other group of black people in the world. The sufferings of his ancestors were inhuman, but they opened the door to a change in the lives of the generations of their children. Uncle Jo told Johnson that in Africa, many parents go the extra mile in their struggle for survival to give their children a chance at a better life. For example, Uncle Jo's father told him that when food is not enough in many African families, the parents of those families would tell their children that they were not hungry. But in actuality, those parents sacrificed their share so that their children would have enough to eat. What Johnson was learning here was that his past has a purpose. Johnson said that he must stop waiting for the white people to undo what they did to his ancestors, which was transferred to him. He started thinking of what to do to enable him to take advantage of the opportunities available to him. He started thinking of finding Africa missing in him.

Uncle Paul acknowledged that the sufferings of Johnson's ancestors in America were inhuman and never before seen anywhere in the world. However, he told Johnson that many Europeans who came to America suffered terrible injustice, prejudice, and discrimination at the hands of their own people before coming to America. Uncle Paul stated that sometimes, bad things happen to good people. However, he argued that if the Europeans who came to America did not suffer terrible injustice from their own people, they might not have come to America for better opportunities. In another dimension, Johnson learned that the Europeans who came to America did not continue to feel bad about the way their parents were treated by their own people. Instead, they reconciled with the European people long ago, moved on, and continued to work together. White people realized that their origin is too important to give up. Uncle Paul pointed out to Johnson that everybody's origin was everybody's roots. No tree grows big and firm without maintaining a secured contact with the ground. Johnson reasoned that it was time to go back to his African roots, make secure contact with African soil, and be able to grow big and stand firm. He realized that there is no substitute for one's roots. For Johnson, success is much more than a good education and financial wealth. Success actually starts with knowing who one is. Johnson believed that without an original identity, one would continue to remain empty inside. It was time to search and find the Africa that was missing in him.

Johnson's relationship with the new African American immigrants. Johnson has a number of friends among the new African American immigrants. On the one hand, he knew that the difference between the new African immigrants and his parents was that the new immigrants came to America of their own free will like all other immigrants from all over the world. Still, the slaves, including his parents, came to America in bondage against their will. On the other hand, he knew that all immigrants have two things in common to all of them. First, in America, immigrants have many opportunities not available in their respective countries of origin. And second, all immigrants came to America to take advantage of the opportunities in America to develop themselves and contribute resources to build America.

However, the new African immigrants did not experience the inhuman suppression and humiliation their parents were subjected to. Johnson was curious to know if there was any difference between his peers among the new immigrants and his peers whose parents were subjected to various social pressures like stripping away of culture, racism, prejudice, discrimination, and many more social problems. He found that the most important difference is that the new African immigrants have original family structures similar to those of their original ancestors who came to America as their own masters. To Johnson, the family is the foundation of human development. The worst thing the early white people did to his family was fdestroyed family structure. This made them start all over to build a new structure based on borrowed values. In addition, among his peers, the new African immigrants, Johnson found that they have less of his kind of problems: they have, by far, lesser school dropouts, appear more patient, often can keep a job, and among women, there are, by far, lesser teenage pregnancies. On a wider scope, Johnson has a problem with one fundamental question—he wanted to know why the Africans sold their brothers and sisters into slavery. Johnson was told that slavery happened as a result of ignorance, stupidity, and sometimes, greed. This answer was not very satisfactory to Johnson, but that did not stop his resolution to recover his ethnicity, because in Johnson's opinion, only that could restore his values of originality. Johnson hoped to learn more about this issue when he got to Africa. Johnson later learned that slavery was not new in the world, including Europe, Africa, and

America. As a matter of fact, many of the original African American ancestors were slaves before they came to America. But what was new was the inhuman treatment imposed on African Americans, subjecting them to a condition unworthy of human beings.

CHAPTER 6

Family Values

Johnson grew up learning what to do and what not to do from interactions with his family members. He understood what behaviors were acceptable and what were not. For example, he learned that his mother was happy when he did positive things that she approved of and unhappy with him with things that she disapproved of. He was taught to respect others, especially adults. As he became older, he asked why he could not do things in other good ways his mother did not dictate. His mother told him that adults know better, and he must learn from them. As time went on, he became more uncomfortable being told what to do and to respond in a particular pattern. At times, he interacted unintentionally in a way he felt acceptable. This made his mother angry. Johnson's mother felt that his behavior should be predictable to adult members of his family. Johnson's family members apparently created a powerful sense of predictability hidden in the silent structure of their family's culture.

His family members' manner of interaction formed a pattern that Johnson was expected to use in his interaction with others. His mother told him that the family's pattern of interaction would help him to understand his family structure. To add to his knowledge about African family structure, Johnson asked his Great-Uncle Jo for the secret of his ancestor's strength. Uncle Jo told him that men were raised as future warriors. This aspect of the African family structure caught his attention. He believed that he had the blood of warriors in his veins. Johnson looked forward to becoming a leader because he believed that all warriors are potential leaders.

According to Dr. Paul, some family structures are rigid and others, like African structures, are diffuse. He said some structure patterns could be too rigid, and some could be too diffuse. Paul told Johnson that a rigid pattern helps one develop independence but could make one less affectionate to the folks around. In contrast, a diffuse family structure would encourage loving and helping others; but this, he said, could be at the expense of one's autonomy. Johnson learned that the rigid structure is a Western culture, and the diffuse pattern is African culture. However, Dr. Paul believed that there is no perfect family structure, but the fact remains that individuals are naturally pulled toward their family structure of origin.

Johnson found himself in between two competing expectations. First was the expectation from his African American background to behave diffusely according to his roots, and second was the expectation from the American society for him to behave rigidly in his relationship with people around him. This was a dilemma for Johnson. If he adopts the rigid Western structure, he would be seen as a white African American person without the roots of his ancestors. On the other hand, if he adopts the diffuse African American structure, the whites, who are in the majority in America, would see him as living a family structure that is foreign to the united all-American culture. Johnson decided to adopt his original African American family structure as a foundation to adjust to his overall American structure. Johnson believed that his decision would enable him to close the hole in him and would help make him a stable person with a high sense of self-concept. Johnson knew that he could never be a typical white person or African person. He wanted to be what is real, an African American person, because it is rooted in the origin of his African ancestors. This would help him to be and to understand exactly who he is. The stability achieved from this decision would enable him to take advantage of the many opportunities available only here in America. But to achieve this goal, he must first find the Africa that is missing in him. Johnson argued that if a new African were to come to America today, with a pillowcase in hand and no money in their pocket and work hard to put themselves into the American mainstream—wash dishes, go to school and graduate, buy a house, marry, and put children to college—but he who is born and raised in America cannot, then something must be fundamentally wrong with him. Johnson resolved that he must nip in the bud whatever the problem was. America is the land of opportunity, and it is up to him to take advantage of the opportunities in America

Johnson's present family structure can be described as unstable. His mother never married, and he does not know who his father is or what he looks like. He learned everything knows about family structure from his mother, from Uncle Jo, and from Dr. Paul. Uncle Jo talked much about the original family structure of Johnson's African ancestors as people whose family structure is stable. Dr. Paul helped Johnson learn about the African American family structure shaped by the early white people. Uncle Jo said that the culture of a people is the basis of a child's socialization. He learned that a child that did not attach and bond with parents has little chance of healthy growth and development." Johnson's sense of family structure was a mixture of the African and American versions. He learned simultaneously, some from family members and some from Dr. Paul. From what Johnson learned, African American ancestors came to America with a family-structure knowledge dated thousands of years ago. Jo told Johnson that when the early white people stripped away the sacred African American structure, the new African American family structure based on borrowed values was created. The African Americans were forced to start from scratch to learn and build a new family structure. Jo believed that if Johnson had his original cultural background, he would have used it as eyes with which to see the white people's family structure and be able to adapt to it. But losing his original cultural background made Johnson blind and unable to see the new white family structure clearly. Johnson could not adjust to the white people's culture. He fumbled into it. Johnson believed that blending his old culture into his new culture could be peaceful and harmonious, unlike fumbling into his new culture. He believed that the fumbling method helped create all sorts of conflicts in his life.

Johnson was very anxious to find out why he was the way he found himself—unhappy, always angry, rebellious, and unable to concentrate. Because Johnson trusted in Dr. Paul's experience, intelligence, and wisdom, Johnson asked Dr. Paul to help him understand the cause of the conflicts in his life. Dr. Paul told Johnson that the answer to his question was very complex. However, he told Johnson that one of the possible ways of looking at his situation was through his life history from conception. He believed that every person's development before birth involves the interactions of the gene and the experiences of the person's parents. For Johnson, this meant that he inherited his parents' experiences of anger, frustration, the effects of the Jim Crow laws, racism (discrimination), the stripping of culture, and many more unjust experiences. Uncle Paul told Johnson that the experiences inherited by a child from the parents are among the reasons why many African parents want to know the past experiences of the bride's and groom's families before blessing the marriage. This is expressed in the African marriage-contracting tradition. Uncle Paul went on to describe a typical African marriage-contracting process.

When a young man finds a girl that he loves and intends to marry, the young man goes home and tells his parents that he found his bride. The groom's parents will express joy and ask who the girl is. Their son will then say who the girl is. The young man's parents will then select a few men, a woman never included, to visit the of the bride-to-be's family. First, one of the few selected men will make a formal appointment by telling the father or an elder among the girl's family that a few of them representing a named family will be visiting the father or the elder's family on an agreed evening. On that day, the few selected men will visit the bride's family, carrying a keg of wine as a sign of goodwill. When this appointment is made, the bride-to-be's family will select a small group waiting to welcome their visitors. When the visitors arrive, they will express themselves as friends in a very cultural manner. The host group will also reciprocate in a very friendly manner. Usually, the host group will feel that the visit has something to do with marriage. But they will never be sure until the visiting group spells out the purpose of the visit. Of course, the host group will present a kola nut to the visiting group as a sign of love and friendship. After a traditional prayer and the breaking and eating of the kola nut, the leader of the visiting group will clear his throat in a smooth, noisy way as a sign to the host group that the visiting group is ready to spell out the purpose of their visit. This lead speaker will always talk in a diplomatically. He may say, "Our son told us that he saw somebody very beautiful in your family." In a second statement, the speaker will then specify by mentioning the name of the host group's daughter. The rest of the visiting group members will then agree or show by body language that the speaker indeed spoke the purpose of their visit. The leader of the host group will then thank the visitors for their nice words about their daughter. This meeting is, indeed, the beginning of the marriage-contract process.

The purpose of this short marriage-contract-process description is to make point out the Africans' belief in the transfer of experiences from the parents to the children. From this stage of the marriage-contract process, each side of the group would do all they can to find information about each other. This meeting of both sides is a preamble to an investigation by each side of each other's family history. Each side wants to know the behavioral history of the other's family. The bride and her family want to know about the young man, his parents, and the rest of his family. The same goes for the young girl. The groom and family want to know about the background of the girl and her family. The investigations aim to know behaviors or experiences in a family that may have been inherited by the young man or young lady at birth or during their life. Each group wants to know as much as possible about each other's family backgrounds. After all, an African proverb says, "A child that does not behave like his father or mother is a stranger in the family." The above marriage-contract preamble is very important. It enables both families to ensure that the marriage is contracted on a solid foundation that would promote the growth of love, morals, and social and economic success in the young marriage. After the investigation stage of the marriage-contract process, each side involved in the marriage process would evaluate the information they collected and decide whether to proceed with the marriage contract. However, it is important to say that the investigations are never made public. In fact, they are done secretly. At this point, each side will be playing a waiting game, looking forward to knowing if the process will continue into the next stage. This expectation is more on the side of the bridegroom-to-be's family because the groom's family usually has the upper hand in influencing the marriage process. If the groom's family feels that the bride's family has a good history of behavioral background, then a messenger is sent to the bride's family to schedule a second meeting. This meeting is a major event. The decision at this meeting is traditionally binding in society. Again, the groom's side will select a group representing the groom's family at the meeting. On the other hand, the bride's side will do the same in selecting a group that would welcome the visitors. The host family will make the necessary preparation. There will be enough food and wine for everybody, the host members and the visitors at the meeting. When the visitors arrive, they will be ushered to a special room prepared for the meeting. The bride's family will be sitting on one side, and the groom's family will be on the other, like Republicans and Democrats in Congress. These two groups will include elders and young men. When all group members are settled in their seats, the elder, usually the oldest among the bride's group, will welcome their visitors. Again, a kola nut will be presented to visitors, and traditional prayers will be said. The kola nut will be broken and eaten. Next, the host group will look up to the visitors to spell out the purpose of their second visit. Accordingly, the leader of the groom's group will clear his throat in smoothly and noisily to signal that his group is ready to declare their intention. The leader of the groom's group will salute the host group in a traditional manner and will thank them for the good welcome they received. This leader will then tell the host group that they were making a second visit because they like what they see in their daughter and that they have come to know what it takes for the host group to give the hands of their daughter to them in marriage. After this speech, the other members of the groom's group would express support to show that their leader had, indeed, spoken the intention of their second visit. Further, the ball would roll over to the court of the host group. The leader of the host group would likely say that his group is proud of their daughter. He may assure the groom's group that their daughter is well socialized and that their daughter is well behaved and highly educated. At this point, the floor is set for discussing the marriage dowry. The dowry is the money paid to the girl's parents for their hard work in training their daughter from birth to maturity. After talking with members of his group to agree on the amount of money demanded from the groom's group, the leader would ask for a saucer. He may place ten pieces of broomsticks in the saucer, and a young man would take the saucer from the leader of the bride's group and would hand it over to the leader of the groom's group. The groom's group would understand that the ten pieces of broomsticks represent ten thousand dollars. The groom's group would likely say they would like to step aside for a short discussion on how to respond. They may decide to respond with four and a half pieces of the broomsticks. In this case, the group would remove five and a half pieces of broomsticks. Then the leader of the groom's side would hand the saucer over to the young man, who would then hand the saucer back to the bride's group. The bride's group may decide to put back two pieces of broomsticks, making what is in the saucer six and a half pieces of broomsticks. Again, the saucer would be handed back to the groom's group. The groom's group may take away a half piece and send back the saucer with six broomsticks. The bride's group may accept and thank them. This means an agreement has been reached, and the dowry is accepted to be six broomsticks, representing six thousand dollars. At this point, the leaders of the bride's group would send for their daughter to go into the meeting room. The mother of the bride would make sure that her daughter is dressed in her best. The girl would report to the leader of her group. The leader would pour wine from a keg into a cup and ask their daughter to walk to the other side and show them who her husband would be by handing over the cup of wine to the man who would be her husband. The girl would walk to her husband-to-be, kneel down, drink some, and hand over the cup of wine to the future husband. The man would accept the cup, drink out of the cup, and hand the cup over to any member of his group.

This ritual indicates that it takes a village to build a successful family. This concludes the agreement that the bride and groom have accepted themselves as husband and wife before both families as witnesses. This agreement is traditionally binding in their society.

Johnson lamented on learning of the importance that his African ancestors placed on the institution of marriage and how all those values were stripped away, resulting in all that he suffered. However, Uncle Paul argued that the American founding fathers intended to create one common ethnicity for all groups from different nations. That seemed to be a perfect idea at the time. They assumed that by the time people from different places intermarry, their children continue the process of intermarriage. The result would be a common ethnic society. Johnson loved that assumption plan because nobody would be identified by color, race, and place of origin. Everybody would have been identified by a single name—American. There would not be black Americans, African Americans, white Americans, Mexican Americans, and so on. Johnson regretted that the American society did not implement the founding fathers' well-intended family plan. The result is that marriage has not been used successfully as a tool for the civilization of races in America.

For Johnson, his family was denied access to the African cultural background. The white men's assumption of using intermarriage to mix and unite all groups has not succeeded. He learned that his African ancestors had high behavioral standards for their children and expected them to keep family values that way. This high expectation is always balanced with constant family group support and affection. Unfortunately, the African extended-family system did not work for Johnson in an American environment. Johnson grew up with no father in his home, which was the same for many of his peers growing up. Johnson's mother was not married, and teenage pregnancy continues to be a big problem for many young women like his mother. Johnson was a school dropout and observed that a high school dropout is common in the African American community. Johnson did not have a prison-time experience, but he learned that about one million African American teenagers are in prison, evidence of low-income family backgrounds and socialization in poverty.

Johnson thought that one of the aspects of the marriage problem for his mother, and many other young black women, was the unavailability of adequate young black men to marry. First is the issue of availability, with many young black men in prison. The next problem is that among the available young black men, many are addicted to drugs and alcohol, and some are mentally ill. Furthermore, Johnson learned that among the few young men who should be husbands to young women, many are either underemployed or unemployed. Because of this, Johnson believed that this is why there are more single parents like his mother, even though those young women want to be married. There are simply more black women than competent black men available for marriage. Johnson remembered what Uncle Jo once told him, that their ancestors who came to America believed that a man must first prove himself competent to be a husband before he gains support from peers and elders to go into marriage. Jo also said that the number one duty of a young man, according to their ancestors' standard, is to provide for the family—provide food, shelter, and security. His ancestors believed that a man should love himself, his family, his neighborhood, his state, and his country.

Further, a typical ancestor young man is a potential warrior, always ready to demand his rights and ready to fight adversaries when necessary to preserve his right and freedom for self, family, state, and country. And a typical ancestor young woman is family-oriented, ready to support her husband and take care of her husband and children. Occasionally, an ancestor young woman could also be a warrior. Johnson lost the above virtues because of the lack of environmental support at home and in the community while growing up. He saw himself easily driven by reactivity to people around him. He positioned himself to blame others instead of seeing himself as a warrior, like his ancestors. He believed that others caused all his problems. Johnson remembered Dr. Paul telling him that people do what they do because of their internal mental state, such as beliefs.

Another aspect of the problem that affected the stability of Johnson's family was the effect of the Jim Crow laws. "But how did these subversive laws come about?" Johnson asked. He learned that these laws started as the African Americans struggled to survive the white government's oppression and suppression and forge agreements with lower-class whites who were poor just like them. Some white people during those days interpreted the agreement between blacks and the lower-class whites as a threat that could lead to blacks and poor whites revolting against the rich white people. To prevent this threat, the whites used their majority power to legislate state laws that included constitutional amendments and city ordinances, making segregation and discrimination practices legal. Johnson learned these laws included the prohibition of interracial marriages and cohabitation. African American children were not allowed to attend school together with white children. And many other laws humiliated, discriminated against, and segregated African Americans. Using these laws, the white people of the slave period reduced the African Americans to the type of whiteness that was not the same as the whiteness of the real white man. In this way, Johnson lost both the original strength of the white culture and the stripped culture of his African ancestors. Johnson concluded that it was in the institution of family that his African American ancestors, including his family, suffered the most indignation. This was more so because the law of the land recognized neither fatherhood nor slave marriagesd. He was told that even though miscegenation was illegal, the white masters did not appear serious about enforcing the law because miscegenation was observed to be common between slave women and white men. Similarly, the same attitude was applied to slave breeding, which became a common means of creating slaves for money after the abolition of the slave trade. Johnson was told that the members of slave families could be separated at the command of the slave owner, and the slave master could rape his women slaves at will.

In Johnson's opinion, he suffered all the above either directly or indirectly. Some he suffered because learning of them caused him serious concern, and some he believed were transferred to him at birth through gene-experience interaction. Uncle Paul told Johnson that the problems of some teenagers like him started early as a result of a lack of bonding and attachment between him and family members, especially bonding between him and his parents. For example, Dr. Paul believed that a healthy relationship during childhood development and, in fact, during adulthood depends on the parents' physical proximity and attachment with the child growing up. Johnson concluded from all he learned that separating black families deprived black parents of the opportunity for parent-child interactions, which could have provided the chance for black parents to learn and improve parenting skills, coping skills, and communication skills. These skills enable parents to socialize with their children to be on good behavior and develop in a healthy manner.

Johnson argued that with the above experiences, it is unfair for anybody to hold parents like his mother and father responsible for the inadequate role they played in raising him. As a result of the above, parents appeared to pass up their responsibilities to other institutions, like schools or the church, instead of seeing themselves as the primary educators of their children. He further argued that he grew up in a situation where government policies directly or indirectly stripped or destroyed the morality of his parents, starting with their African American ancestors. The government then turned around and blamed his parents for not socializing with him well. He believed that his mother's teenage pregnancy and his father not being there for him were not all the faults of his parents but those of the racists' government policies. He his parents' behaviors were the unforeseen contingencies created by government policies of the past slave period. However, Johnson resolved that he would not live as his parents did. There is a sense of urgency for him to find the Africa that was stripped away from his ancestors and passed on to him. As he learned, it is time for him to take advantage of the freedom and liberty of the American constitution—the best in the world.

CHAPTER 7

The Discovery of Self

Johnson set out to know how he came about being often angry. He continued his habit of asking questions and, sometimes, finding answers. Some of his findings made him conclude that his angry behavior, according to Uncle Jo, stemmed from the anger of his ancestors since the day they were forced against their will into the ship away from their homeland to America. When they arrived in America, they were made angrier when their sacred way of life was stripped away. This change in their lifestyle was interpreted as a taboo in the African culture. To help them cope, they adopted a new way of life that facilitated their ability to survive all kinds of social pressures inflicted on them by the slave masters. Uncle Jo said that Johnson's ancestors were socialized as poor and uneducated, but their new-culture value system enabled them to be a support group to one another. This new lifestyle was very helpful because the stripping of their cultural strength translated into a loss of their natural ability to cope with worry and other troubles that resulted from discrimination, prejudice, and racism. Their group support was very helpful but not enough for major problems. The unintended consequences of their loss were enormous stress, anxiety, depression, and other emotional disorders. Johnson's ancestors were forced to live their lives doing wearisome manual labor in very unhealthy working conditions. Some of them and their children did this all through their lifetime. This condition created hopelessness, and for many, like Johnson's parents, their lives were subjected to chains of disorganized lifestyle. As a result, the members of their ethnic group continued to adjust to a culture of pain, fear, and servitude. But behind their pretense was a big hole of dissatisfaction. This was the environment in which Johnson was raised.

When Johnson took a second look at his experience, he perceived awareness of the liberty offered to his parent by the white masters after many years of oppression and suppression. Unfortunately, they became free of slavery but continued to complain and held on to the expectation of the white masters to undo the psychological damage done to them. This is the point where Johnson decided to be different from his parents. He realized that he was free to reconstruct his cultural base. He made a conscious decision not to live as his parents did. For him, a gift of freedom was like a second chance in life. He believed that when given lemons, one needs to make lemonade. In Johnson's opinion, the reconstruction of his cultural life is similar to making lemonade. He felt that the opportunities in America that are not available in other countries are too precious to forgo by not doing whatever it takes to achieve change. Johnson decided to make a change instead of continuing to complain over things that happened hundreds of years ago. Johnson chose to count himself lucky to be born in America. He preferred to change and take advantage of the good life America offers to those who can believe in themselves. Johnson saw a sense of urgency and a need for him to change now. He decided that he must change and resolved to go back to the origin, make contact with it, and regain his originality. He must go back to Africa to reunite with his roots. This, he believed, would help him close the hole in his heart. To Johnson, no amount of talking with white people would do this for him. He understood that his problem was behavioral and that only he could make the change he needed. Johnson intended to travel to the village from which his ancestors came hundreds of years ago. His first problem was how to locate the village of his ancestors.

One night when Johnson was sleeping, Uncle Jo appeared to him and talked about the New Yam Festival in the Ozuzumba village. He said that Johnson could not achieve stability until he regained his originality. Johnson woke up wondering what New Yam Festival meant. He quickly recalled two things—Uncle Jo used to talk about festivals in Africa and that their ancestors came from the Ozuzumba village. This was probably the most important piece of information he learned from his uncle. Johnson remembered that Jo used to talk of their ancestors being very brave warriors on the war front. Their ancestors were great farmers. The New Yam Festival was an annual thanksgiving celebration in which the village people thanked their god for blessing them with a great harvest. Uncle Jo's appearance to Johnson in the dream made him think of how complex the universe is. Johnson felt that human beings start their journey in the world at their roots, and when people die, they return to their roots, where they began. He felt this way because Johnson could not understand how his uncle, who died years ago, appeared to him in a dream, talking about his participation in the New Yam Festival. However, Johnson was not certain about his interpretation of his dream. He said to himself that he would clarify this information when he travels to Africa. Now that Johnson knew the name of shis ancestors' village, he had to check with the embassies of West African countries in America for the location of the Ozuzumba village in Africa. Johnson had no idea what Ozuzumba looked like, but the wealth of information he acquired from Uncle Jo made Johnson feel like he had been there before. Uncle Jo was able to talk about ancient events or information about them because he was somebody who loved to stay around old relatives—his father, grandfather, uncles, and great-uncles. Johnson valued these pieces of information as great assets worth more than money. For Johnson, these assets contain information that would help him change hundreds of years of problems he inherited from his parents.

At last, the time came for Johnson to implement the resolution he promised himself—going back to the origin to regain originality and finding the Africa that was missing in him. Johnson wanted this trip to Africa so bad because he was convinced that his white friends wished that he could rediscover himself. This, they hoped, would help Johnson relate or interact with them with his full potential as a stable person. They believed that Johnson's cultural strength would enable him to understand who he was. This information, they believed, would empower Johnson to contribute his best toward the building of America. Johnson believed that his contributions would enable him to achieve his American dream.

When he searched for information about Ozuzumba, he learned about their king, EbubeDike, whose name means "the pride of a warrior." Johnson sent a mail to the king telling him who he was and of his intention to trace the original home of his ancestors. King EbubeDike received the mail and expressed excitement. He gave the news to his cabinet members and his family. The king replied to Johnson's letter and included his phone number. When Johnson sent the mail, he was unsure how the king would receive his request. However, when Johnson received a reply from the king, it was one of the happiest days of his life. Johnson waited four days, put his thoughts together, and made a phone call to the king. When the king's private phone rang, he took the call, praised Johnson for his courage, and told Johnson that his palace, his cabinet, and his people were all looking forward to celebrating his visit and his unification with the roots of his ancestors. The king told

Johnson that his tribe's people say, *"When a child is crying and pointing in a particular direction, the child's father, mother, or both must be in a location in that direction."* The king told Johnson that when he decided on the date to visit, he should call and inform him. The date should be, say, one month ahead of time. After about three months, Johnson called King EbubeDike, the people's king, and announced that he would visit in one month. When the king received the information, he summoned the members of his cabinet and spoke to them about the great news. The king unveiled the whole story about Johnson. He is the son of one of their great warriors who was captured by their enemies during one of their intertribal wars many years ago. He told the cabinet members that Johnson would be visiting from America to trace the roots of his ancestors who were sold into slavery by their adversaries. After deliberations with his cabinet, the king announced that during Johnson's visit, there would be rituals in atonement for his people's weakness in allowing their warriors to be captured. There would also be a great celebration for the survival of the descendant of their great warrior.

The king deliberated about Johnson's visit with his cabinet members. After the deliberation, the king decreed that every adult male and household would donate food (yam, cocoyam, chickens, and goats). The king volunteered to donate all the cows needed for the celebration. Next, all age grades would be ready with their dances and masquerades—Ijele (the biggest and the most beautiful), Enweaka (masquerade with no hands), Oji-Onu, Etili-ogwu, and other dances and masquerades. There would also be women's dances and children's performances. The king expanded his entertainment square and renovated the palace in preparation for the coming celebration. As the big day came closer, the town crier went out in the night to announce that the celebration day was getting closer to remind all groups to be ready for their participation.

The king ordered special costumes for himself, members of the royal family, and members of his cabinet.

Similarly, the members of different groups that would be participating ordered costumes for the celebration. The costumes were made to fit the occasion. This celebration was the first of its kind, which is why it was given special attention. The king invited other kings and chiefs from various neighboring towns and villages. In turn, each of the towns and villages that were invited prepared entertainment groups to present performances of their choice at the celebration. This was a hundreds-of-years-old celebration. The king told Johnson his age-grade group would present him with their dance to the village community.

Johnson knew that a trip to Africa would be a ritual of his lifetime. He was going to do what he felt some in his ethnic group might have thought of doing but never did, probably because they were afraid or decided to settle for less by accepting the values the white people gave them. They behaved in a manner that would make them acceptable to society. In Johnson's opinion, they chose to be American Africans. As part of Johnson's preparation, he worked very hard, took two jobs to raise money pay for his flight, and bought lots of things he would give away as gifts to people who would welcome him there in Africa. As the date of Johnson's travel came closer and closer, time also seemed to run faster and faster. Johnson communicated his travel arrangement to the king: his time of departure from America and his time of arrival in Africa. Finally, the date of his journey came. Johnson dressed in blue jeans, T-shirt, and canvas basketball shoes. He dressed simply because he was told that the weather was hot in Africa. He prepared merely as he did not take with him many changes of clothes. Johnson was nervous because he did not know how the people of Ozuzumba would receive him. His mother and some friends dropped him at the airport and wished him a safe journey and good luck. He checked into the plane with only one piece of luggage. When departure time came, Johnson's plane lifted off the ground into the air to Africa.

Inside the plane, Johnson kept thinking of how the king and the people of Ozuzumba would receive him. There were many white people on the plane visiting Africa. Johnson asked himself why more white people than African Americans like him were visiting Africa. Some Africans were visiting or returning to their homeland. Johnson was the only African American on the plane going to Africa. He was thinking about whom the white people owould visit in Africa and why white people seem to have more interest in Africa, the home of his ancestors, than African Americans like him have. A white man was sitting beside him, and Johnson asked whom he would visit. The white man told him that he was going on a business trip. The businessman told Johnson that Africa was virgin land for business and that the African Americans did not know what they were missing by not connecting with their place of origin. The white man told Johnson that all other people in America—the Jews, the Europeans, the Asians—connect with their various places of origin. These other Americans use their advantage of being citizens of America (the richest country in the world) to do business with the countries of their ancestral origin. The white man asked Johnson if he was also on a business trip or a vacation. Johnson told him that he was making a trip of a lifetime, that he was going to find Africa. The white man asked him, "What do you mean?" Johnson told the white man that the average white man would not understand what it means to ship Africans to America and strip away all the values of their cultural origin. Johnson said that the loss of originality created a hole in him growing up. And then came a sense of urgency to bring closure to this hole. In his opinion, this hole in him has influenced how he interacts with white people and, in fact, with fellow black Americans. He believed that after his ritual trip to Africa, he would return to America as a stable, proud, self-confident, and color-blind African American. The white man admired what looked like a sense of wisdom and told Johnson his thought might be a key to solving the differences between blacks and whites in America.

After many hours of express flight, Johnson's plane touched ground in Ozuzumba, Africa. The king of Ozuzumba and his men made arrangements to receive Johnson from the airport to the king's palace. The king is a wealthy man, even though many of his subjects are poor; however, the people of Ozuzumba are hardworking. They are contented, proud, and self-sufficient. Johnson's flight was long. About halfway into his journey, Johnson fell asleep. He was still sleeping when his plane touched the ground in Africa. A flight attendant touched him and informed him they had reached their destination. Johnson woke up, and stretched. He walked out of the plane, holding a signboard high with *Johnson* written on it. The king's men saw Johnson's sign, walked straight to him, shook his hand, and welcomed him to Ozuzumba. They picked up Johnson's luggage and proceeded to a long black Mercedes-Benz stretch limousine with a driver waiting for Johnson. As Johnson and the king's men approached the black limousine, Johnson asked himself, "Is this waiting for me?" He saw himself elevated to a position of importance. He felt welcomed like a prince. From this moment, Johnson felt different—proud, confident, and happy. Johnson said, "I was never this happy in my life." For him, this experience translated into high self-esteem and a positive self-concept. Johnson entered the limousine, and the driver took off to the king's palace, where the king and the members of his cabinet were waiting to welcome him. A couple of miles to the palace, a traditional talking trumpet sounded, saying that the lost prince was coming home. A dance group by the name of Igba-Dike (the drum for warriors), made up of able-bodied men dressed in traditional regalia, was dancing toward the limousine to welcome Johnson.

Johnson was amazed at the pomp and pageantry he was being welcomed. All along in America, Johnson felt that he was nobody. To be welcomed like a prince was beyond his imagination. He could not contain the happiness that overwhelmed him. At one point, Johnson told the limo driver to stop. The driver stopped, and Johnson went out of the limousine. He started dancing to the tune of the drums. The precision in Johnson's dance made the drummers conclude that Johnson is really one of them. It was a great day for Johnson. He felt himself touching and embracing Africa. The talking drum was calling on their ancestors to go and welcome their son. As they danced into the palace, where the king and cabinet were waiting, they nodded their heads in agreement that Johnson was the son of their ancient warrior. As the drummers approached the threshold of the palace, the king stood up, walked toward Johnson, and embraced him. The king ordered the guards to usher Johnson into the costume room, where Johnson was dressed in befitting princely clothes. After being dressed, he was escorted to a vast circular parlor where the king, his cabinet members, and the elders of Ozuzumba were waiting to perform rituals in appeasement of God.

At the ritual ceremony, one of the oldest among the elders stood up, cleared his throat in a traditional way, and started talking in the Ozuzumba language, thanking God for preserving Johnson. They thanked God for guiding Johnson back to the soil of his ancestors. They prayed that Johnson would have a long life, marry, and be blessed with children, boys and girls. They prayed that Johnson would live long and become a successful, great man. After the prayers, all the elders, including the king, responded with one voice, "Iseee." This response meant that all that the elders prayed for would come to pass. Next, the king, the elders, and Johnson all moved to an entertainment square for eating, drinking, and dancing. At the end of the reception ceremony, the king announced a date for the welcome ceremony for Johnson. In that ceremony, all the citizens of Ozuzumba, the invited kings of neighboring towns and their entourage, and entertainment groups would participate. After a couple of hours, the reception ceremony ended, and Johnson was escorted to a suite made up of rooms and a big parlor where he was to stay throughout his visit.

When Johnson arrived at the king's palace, he was dumbfounded. Johnson never expected to find mansions in the village in Africa. Johnson was born into poverty and grew up with the wrong information that there is nothing good about Africa. For him, it would be a matter of double jeopardy for a poor person like him to identify himself with poor Africa, as he previously learned. To him, this was so because of the many negative things that Johnson heard some white folks talk about Africa; for example, Africa was described as a jungle where danger and misery were the norms. Johnson was ashamed of identifying himself with his roots. It required much information and education from Uncle Jo and his friend Dr. Paul to change his mind about Africa. When Johnson arrived in the king's palace, he discovered that more than one-half of what Africa is was lost in what he was told about Africa back in America. Before taking this trip, Dr. Paul reminded him to always remember while in Africa that he is an American from the most powerful country in the world. Dr. Paul said this to Johnson because, as an intellectual person, he knew that Johnson would discover facts that may not agree with what he learned from some white folks in America. When Johnson decided to travel to Africa, he looked forward to learning as much as possible. After settling down, Johnson requested assistance to enable him to see the village. His peers walked him into the village every morning to see it and learn about the people of Ozuzumba.

One of the reasons why Johnson went to his roots was to find out why people from other poor countries came to America and behaved happier, more organized, and eventually became more successful than him, who was a born-and-raised citizen of the richest and most powerful country in the world. Johnson asked one of his peers why they appeared happy even though many of them were poor. The Ozuzumba peer told Johnson that, by tradition, the young Ozuzumba person is always grateful to parents for whatever parents could give to the individual through education and cultural values. The young Ozuzumba person believes that the sky is the limit of success, that whatever a young person wants and does not get from parents, they must work hard and achieve what they desire. This is one of the reasons why they are called warriors. They do not give in to what they want. They persevere, work hard, believe in themselves, and succeed. They must be happy with what they have and work hard for what they want.

Johnson adjusted himself to his new environment. He was not shy. He learned a few words of the Ozuzumba language within a short time. He asked questions, and his peers, friendly, explained whatever Johnson wanted to know. The king's guards were more than happy for Johnson to want to know and understand the basic values of his roots. After about one week, Johnson told his peers he needed no more assistance. He walked the streets by himself. When Johnson walked along the village streets, he saw the same activities that function in America: schools, markets, farming, businesses, and the transportation system. The difference is high technology with which activities were performed quickly and more efficiently in America. Johnson turned around and asked himself, "Who said that black people are lazy?" as some folks in America say. After observing how hardworking the Africans were, Johnson confirmed that the original reason black people were forced to America was that Africans were very hardworking and very resistant to odd situations and conditions. According to Dr. Paul, this was why the slaves were able to contribute about one-tenth of the American wealth with their forced free labor.

Johnson saw originality, felt originality, and regained originality. When Johnson walked along the neighborhood during morning hours, he observed that there were no children of school age walking around. One morning, when Johnson was walking through the neighborhood, he saw a seventy-year-old grandmother walking a crying grandson to school with a small twig in her hand. Johnson stopped them and asked why the child was crying. The grandmother told Johnson that she was walking her grandson to school. She told Johnson that the child did not want to go to school. The grandmother told Johnson that a child that does not want to go to school would not live in her home. In a short conversation, she told Johnson that another of her grandchildren refused to go to school, and she had to spank him and walk him to school every morning. After one week of the morning ritual, the boy fell in love with the school. She was proud to tell Johnson that the said grandson became one of the few doctors in the Ozuzumba village. Johnson saw that going to school is like a religion in Ozuzumba. He pictured a reason why his friends among new African Americans hardly drop out of school. The people of Ozuzumba have much respect for an educated person. The king himself told Johnson in one of their conversations that he studied in London, England, and holds a bachelor's degree in law. When Johnson heard the king talk about the importance of education, he said that the first thing he would do when he returned to America was go back to school and graduate. Education, the king told him, is the key to success.

The people of Ozuzumba have much regard for their ancestors' courage and gallant behavior. They never give in to their desires because of challenging conditions. The king told Johnson that it was the duty of his age-grade group to socialize him into a personality that befits his ancestors. Johnson participated in a number of ritualistic activities, including hunting, dancing, singing, wrestling contests, eating food and drinking palm wine, and many others. The ritualistic activities were used to prepare Johnson for the coming celebration that the king was organizing for Johnson's coming to find his roots. One of the ritualistic activities is the masquerade ritual. This is a very important ceremony in which a young man is initiated into a respected rank in the community. This order gives a young man the right to stand in front of a masquerade or dance with a masquerade in a public square. Women are not allowed to take this order, except, rarely, older women about eighty years old. No woman or man who is not initiated can walk by himself or herself across an open square where a masquerade is performing without being escorted by a man who has been initiated into the masquerade order. Because Johnson was not born in Ozuzumba, it was essential that he must be initiated into the order. Johnson was initiated the night before the great ceremony. During the eve of the celebration, the group of selected young and some elderly men decided on a location where the initiation would take place. Johnson knew that he would be initiated into the masquerade order but did not know what to expect. The Ozuzumba people believe that what is inside the masquerade is the spirit of a dead person and not somebody alive. So, the masquerade initiation reveals to Johnson what is inside a masquerade. This revelation is intended to be a secret.

After Johnson was initiated, he was instructed never to say, whatever was revealed to him, especially in the presence of women. The Ozuzumba village believes that the masquerades came from the grave inside the ground, and after the performance, they would go back into the grave. During the night of the ritual, Johnson was taken to the appointed location and told that some scary—ugly masquerades—would come out from inside the ground by midnight and perform through the night into the following morning. When dawn came, Johnson was escorted to where the masquerades were assembled, and the masquerades revealed themselves. This initiation qualified Johnson to participate in dancing and singing with the masquerades during the celebration. He became accepted and respected as a courageous young Ozuzumba man. He felt proud and self-confident, especially around his peers.

CHAPTER 8

The Celebration

At last, the eve of the celebration came. During the early hours of the night, the town crier went around the town, announcing into the air and reminding people that the long-awaited day had come. All business transactions were closed to enable people to participate because the king decreed. The following day, everybody in the king's palace dressed in a special garment. The people's event center had a specially designed section for the king and his family, his cabinet members, and the dignitaries that the king invited for the occasion. As time was getting closer for the celebration to start, the center was already full of people from the villages and invitees from neighboring towns and villages. Shortly before it was time to start, the king and his entourage, including Johnson, arrived in a convoy of black limousines. When people heard that King EbubeDike was in the event center, they knew it was time to start. After the next few minutes, one of the king's cabinet members officiating as the master of the ceremony (MC) made an announcement informing the crowd of people waiting that the great event was about to start. Honorable Ichie Nnaji Nwokeocha, the master of ceremony, studied in America and held a master's degree in public administration. The king appointed Ichie Nwokeocha as the master of the ceremony because he believed that Nwokeocha's educational background and experience had prepared him the best for the position. First, before the king's speech to declare the celebration open, the MC called on the traditionally appointed high priest to conduct cultural rituals and prayers to appeal to the creator of the universe for peace and harmony throughout the celebration. This involved the breaking of kola nuts and the pouring of palm wine on the ground. Then came the opening speech of the king.

The king stood up and greeted his people and friends in a traditional way. "On behalf of the Ozuzumba people, I welcome you all to this historic celebration. Today, we are gathered here at the people's cerebration center to honor our surviving son, Johnson. He is visiting his ancestors' place of origin in America to recover the roots of his fathers that were stripped away by force from his ancestors by slave masters in America. This status of cultural deficiency was transferred from generation to generation of African Americans and now to Johnson. The first time a celebration of this magnitude was held was during the reign of my great-grandfather, who was one of the bravest of Ozuzumba kings. It was a celebration of victory that marked the end of our twenty-year war with our adversaries, the Umumbas. As you all know from our history, the Ozuzumba people may have lost some battles, but we never suffered defeat in any war. This is why we are called great warriors. Our grandson, Johnson, is the surviving son of one of our great warriors who was taken captive in one of our lost battles with our neighboring adversaries. Hundreds of years ago, the white people bought their ancestors as slaves to work in American plantations. His ancestors were the greatest of Ozuzumba warriors. The battle in which his ancestors were captured was fought on dangerous terrain. Today, Johnson has demonstrated tremendous courage, intelligence, and bravery in locating the origin of his ancestors and visiting home to recover his roots. His visit speaks for itself that, indeed he is a cheap of his father—an Ozuzumba warrior. We have not seen this kind of bravery since his ancestors. This is why I, Eze EbubeDike of Ozuzumba, am hosting this level of celebration to evoke the memory of the gallantry and courage of our warrior fathers to enable Johnson to reactivate the originality that is embedded inside him. We believe that after this visit, Johnson would return to America able to successfully control every condition, situation, and environment in which he may find himself, like a warrior that he is."

At this point, the king took a deep breath and saluted his people again. "Ozuzumba people, Kwenu,"

The people responded, "Yaa, Kwenu, Yaa Kwenu, Yaa."

The king asked his people, "Have I spoken the truth?"

And the crowd responded in affirmation, "Yaa."

The king then continued, "I ask you, all my people and friends, to relax and enjoy this historic celebration of courage, intelligence, and bravery. There is plenty to eat and drink for everybody participating in this celebration. There are all kinds of entertainment groups ready to make this event a joyous day to remember. We look forward to celebrating Johnson's visit, a warrior like his ancestors. You are all welcome again to the people's palace."

As the king finished his speech, all the chiefs and elders stood up, bowed to the king, and saluted him by his traditional title, Eze EbubeDike. From this point, the celebration was officially declared open. All the dancers and masquerades were called into the entertainment amphitheater as scheduled to perform to please the king, his family, cabinet members, guests, and the Ozuzumba people. The first event was from a group described as power-style dancers. It was made up of healthy, muscular young men. The point section of this group came in first, singing and playing musical instruments ranging from drums (*igba*), *ogene*, and *oja* to other minor instruments. When these instruments were played, the music communicated mystery to the dancers, reminding them that, at last, the long-awaited great day had come.

The music tells the power dancers that they are great men like their ancestors and calls on them to come out in a great way and show great demonstrations. The dancers then surged, running, jumping, and tumbling into the event ground, dancing and performing in a very artistic and cultural manner. The drummers followed the dancers behind, not so close, as the dancers performed vigorously in all parts of the event ground. Johnson was told that this dance style is culturally designed to give a warm-up effect to the celebration and to get it started in a very active and energetic manner. The group performed to show that they are strong young warriors. The next group was made up of mature young women. This group's dance style can be described as soft and hard. The women were dressed in beautiful cultural fashion intentionally designed to exhibit beauty and allow agility during dancing. This dance was called Ukwe and was the oldest women-dance style in the Ozuzumba village. The Ozuzumba history says that this dance is hundreds of years old. The women used the dance to show pride and cultural originality and displayed art and power in their style of dancing. The next group, called the Atilogwu dance group, was one of the many other dance groups that kept the crowd screaming and asking for more.

Johnson commented that he could stay all day long, enjoying their magnificent display of acrobatics, music, and costume. This dance group performed in sections of boys and girls of age grades. Johnson said he was having fun that he had never imagined. Then came the dance group that woke up Johnson's feelings of love and lovemaking. This dance was called the Jigida dance. This group was made up of very beautiful young girls about the age of Johnson. They dressed and performed to externalize the beauty of a woman, dancing with pride and confidence. They usually perform on very special occasions and often in functions attended by upper-class dignitaries. The group members are often young, educated, and culturally classed. To be accepted in this dance group, a girl must pass the traditional expectation of a single girl being culturally preserved. The dance group's costume included a short top designed with beads to cover the breast area and a similar matching design worn around the waist to cover the pubic area of a girl.

Johnson was told that girls who participate in this dance usually use their beautiful looks and performance to attract eligible young men to choose them as future wives. Johnson was extremely attracted to some of the girls in the group, but unfortunately, Johnson's mission transcends love issues. Johnson was in Africa to discover his origin. To Johnson, finding Africa brings him a feeling of self-concept and increases his self-esteem. In his opinion, meaningful success in life starts from the inside to the outside. However, Johnson socialized with some of the beautiful girls in his private suite in a very pleasurable manner. In Johnson's opinion, the Jigida dance added much color and pleasure to his welcome celebration.

As the time came for Johnson's presentation by members of his age grade, Johnson left his sitting position within the king's family to join his age grade. Johnson changed from his princely costume to the special outfit designed for him by his age-grade group. They were eagerly getting ready for this main event of the celebration. The main event was obviously the cultural presentation of Johnson to the Ozuzumba people. His group ushered him into the celebration square with a warrior dance (the drum dance for warriors). As Johnson and his age group entered the celebration center, the crowd screamed like never before. Many in the crowd, especially young girls, were standing up, jumping on their legs, stretching, and wishing to be allowed to touch Johnson. Shortly after their entrance, the Ozuzumba masquerades high priest took center stage and issued a traditional command. This brought all other musical instruments to a standstill and allowed the masquerade flutist to talk to their ancestors in a traditional way. The flutist used the wooden flute (*oja*) to communicate to their long-passed-away ancestors, reminding them how respected and great they were when they were alive. The language from the *oja* emotionally drove the dancers wild beyond measure. The *oja* ritual is used to transform performers into their spiritual selves.

When performers are in this mode, they exhibit magical powers. As observed by Johnson, when a performer under the influence pointed to a palm tree and said some words, the palm tree shrank and died immediately. However, as a general rule, powerful masquerades do not use their destructive magical powers when they participate in celebrations for happy occasions, like Johnson coming home to his roots. The flutist invited their ancestors to come and join them in celebrating the visit and the courage demonstrated by their grandson Johnson in coming from America to find his African roots. In the next few minutes, something very extraordinary happened: the flute's incantations evoked the masquerades underground and woke them up in their sleep. The entertainment square was jam-packed with masquerades wearing different costumes. Some of them were very beautiful, but many looked ugly and very scary. They kept popping up from underground as if they were resurrecting. They were colorful and event befitting. This miraculous response to ecstatic invitation demonstrated the effect of the *oja* ritual. The masquerades lined up left and right of Johnson and danced toward the king sitting with his family, cabinet members, and important dignitaries invited to this celebration—the first of its kind and magnitude in modern times. As the dancers went close to the king and cabinet's location, the king's men stood up and welcomed the dancers in the usual Ozuzumba way. The king ordered his men to give to the different dance groups cows, kegs of wine, and cases of alcoholic drinks in appreciation for their participation. Johnson danced side by side with the masquerades to show the Ozuzumba community that he, indeed, was one of the young Ozuzumba warriors. He felt pumped up into a different him. For Johnson, this moment created an insight into wholeness, confidence, and high self-concept. He felt something new—a sense of completeness. He recaptured his lost originality. He found Africa. Johnson felt his recovery of self and a new life inside him. He felt utterly free, happy, and strong. The celebration lasted all day and, finally, came to an end.

That night, after the celebration, Johnson went into his luxurious suite in the king's palace happy like never before in his life. Why was Johnson so happy? one may ask. Johnson felt the emotional awareness of mind and body liberation in his heart. Throughout his life, the anger from the effects of slavery appeared to follow him all works of his life. But when he found Africa, Johnson felt the highest respect he would ever imagine in his life. The celebration of Johnson finding Africa took command as the biggest story in African news and also made front-page news in world history news reports during that month. As Johnson lay down on the bed, looking up to the ceiling, he reviewed his life experiences and found himself a lucky young man. He thanked God for giving him the courage to make his journey to Africa and find himself. He said to himself that if he had not made his journey, he would never have been able to know his worth in his lifetime. He discovered that the Africans who sold his ancestors were the people that loved him most in the world. The white people who enslaved his ancestors provided him the best opportunity for success—opportunities that are not available to any black group in the world. Apparently, Johnson used the two sources of his success to building walls against his happiness. He could not understand this irony. How can someone clever be called stupid? That night, he made a conscious decision that he must forgive the Africans involved in selling his ancestors and the white people who enslaved them. He decided to change the negative feelings in his mind to positive behavior. The negative emotions were like a huge stone holding him down. And then, when he pushed the obstacle out of his way, he felt liberated, optimistic, and happy. At this point, Johnson was ready to return to America—a journey he called his second coming to America.

Johnson has now received the power of positive change. In his new life, he no longer thinks of slavery and the inhuman treatment perpetrated on his ancestor. He is a new person. Johnson has recovered the Africa missing in him. Now that Johnson had found Africa, the question became what to do with his new self. Johnson expressed gratitude to the king, the king's family, the cabinet, his age grade, and the Ozuzumba community. He promised the king and his age group that he would continue to visit from time to time.

As Johnson prepared to return to America, the king and the community donated gifts to Johnson to give to members of his family and friends in America. At this point, Johnson sent a message to his mother and friends, informing them of his return to America. On the eve of Johnson's travel, the king and the cabinet conducted rituals and prayers for Johnson, assuring him that the Ozuzumba soil, ancestors, and people will always support his endeavors for success. The oldest man in the community led the prayers and spoke to their creator in their native language, saying that a great success awaited Johnson in America. The senior leader, Eze Nwokebia, advised Johnson to visit often. Johnson thanked the king and the Ozuzumba people and promised to return to America and display Africa in his daily functioning. Johnson felt his going back to America was a second coming. This time, he made a conscious decision to come to America like every other immigrant who became an American citizen, to take advantage of all the opportunities in

America, develop himself, and contribute his resources toward building America. This mindset gave Johnson a sense of real equality with white people and other people from other cultural backgrounds.

Johnson was coming back color-blind. His flight was scheduled to take off at 11:00 p.m. American time. Johnson packed his load and gifts, and he was ready for the trip back to America. Johnson was wearing a beautiful African dress. The king's limousine took him back to the airport. Some members of the king's cabinet and many from his age grade were there to bid him a safe journey. At 11:00 p.m., his plane lifted off the ground to America. His plane flew express, and Johnson was back in America by morning the following day. His mother and friends welcomed him back.

CHAPTER 9

Johnson and His Return to America

J ohnson came back from Africa a transformed person. He described his return as his second coming to America and he came back with his mind set for success. Perhaps, the most important aspect of his mindset was that he replaced his old identity, which strongly demanded him to accept white superiority while seeing himself as inferior, with a color-blind attitude, believing in himself with the sky as the limit to his success. He now has a positive self-concept, can compete no matter how difficult a situation, and is a young man who believes in himself. As he was growing up, his mother taught him the importance of education, and in school, the teachers made an effort to help him stay in school and learn. Unfortunately, none of these two attempts appeared to work for Johnson, as he dropped out of school. But after observing a seventy-year-old grandmother who woke up early every school day to walk her grandchild to school against the child's desire, at last, Johnson's attention on the importance of education was captured. Another aspect of Johnson's new mindset was the cultural values concerning family responsibilities he learned from his peers during his trip to Africa. Johnson remembered his peers in Ozuzumba telling him that an individual is responsible for their success. They told him that an individual should be grateful for whatever help they get from parents to help the individual succeed and that it is the individual's responsibility to work hard and achieve anything desired that the individual could not get from their parents. This responsibility assumes that an individual is not handicapped by illness or other types of deprivations, man-made or by natural disasters. Johnson argued that if his peers can achieve their dreams in a poor village like Ozuzumba by working hard, he has no excuse whatsoever for failure in America with all kinds of opportunities. Johnson's immediate ambition was to go back to college, graduate, and establish a stable family.

However, Johnson has a new problem—how to relate with peers of his ethnicity who do not have experience of his transformation. He could now connect and interact well with his white peers equally. Johnson's black peers now saw him as trying to be in favor of white people. Johnson said that his white friends now appeared to accept him more as equal. Johnson's black peers still see Johnson as playing white. They felt that Johnson is simply abandoning his ethnicity and joining the white ethnicity. However, what was important for Johnson was what he saw when he looked at himself in the mirror. Johnson said that he sees himself as a new offspring of his African ancestors. In Johnson's opinion, he sees in himself what his friend Dr. Paul saw in the original African ancestors who came to America as their own masters. Johnson was not frustrated at the behavior of some of his black brothers. Instead, he looked forward to finding a way to enable any other "Johnson" to find Africa. The more Johnson was assimilated into the white ethnicity, the more many of his folks saw him as abandoning them. For Johnson, the divide between him and his black brothers created a painful experience. However, he could understand the frustration of his folks because he has been where they have not been. In other words, they do not have his transformation experience. Many of Johnson's white friends were equally frustrated as they could not understand why their peers among black folks could not get over the injustice, prejudice, discrimination, and racism that the slave masters perpetuated during slavery to black people hundreds of times years ago. For Johnson, he knew that his white friends could never understand accurately the effects of unjust laws that caused the children of his ancestors to be born into poverty.

Similarly, Johnson did not expect his white friends to understand why or how the unjust situation experiences made many black children develop abnormally from childhood into adulthood. Nevertheless, Johnson feels that the more important issue is the sense of urgency to do whatever it takes to achieve change and put an end to the transfer of failure from generation to generation. It is time to bring closure to the emptiness. It is time to find Africa that is missing in people like him. However, Johnson said that things need to come first; he must go back to college and develop himself by taking advantage of the opportunities available to him in America. He must first help himself because Johnson remembers an African proverb that says, "A man that is standing on one leg does not dance the music that is meant for people standing on two legs."

Johnson dropped out of college during his second year, but he went back and stayed in school. He worked hard and graduated with his bachelor's degree. He had always wanted to be a lawyer. He applied for admission to law school and was denied. Johnson believed that a law degree would enable him to help less privileged people, and it would be an excellent tool to get into politics. Johnson did not take no for an answer to his application for admission. He applied for admission into a graduate school and was admitted. In two years, he earned a master's degree. This was a more competitive position to reapply for law school admission. This time, Johnson was not only accepted, but he also had the option to choose which school to attend. He chose one of the most prestigious law schools in America. He worked hard through law school and graduated with honors. Johnson was thrilled. He could now see clearly the difference between his life before his trip to Africa and his life after his trip.

Before his trip, Johnson struggled to shake off the identity imposed on him as an African American—the negative stereotypes of society expecting him to accept a second-class position and recognize the white person as his superior. His struggle to shake off his old identity put him in trouble in school and at the workplace. In contrasthe regained his wholeness as an original African American after his trip. To Johnson, it was imperative for him to travel to Africa to regain what he felt was missing in him. But his folks do not understand that he is now a color-blind individual. This does not mean that Johnson thinks that he is a white person. Instead, it meant that Johnson now sees black and white as all beautiful, original colors. Johnson's white friends observed that he directly relates and interacts with them as equals now. Many of his white friends could not understand what happened in Johnson, but they enjoyed the new development in Johnson. Some of Johnson's white friends, who were used to the feeling of superiority, do not appear to like the change in Johnson. They seem to want Johnson to continue to be the old Johnson accepting inferior identity. These white peers still want to put social pressure on Johnson. This became a test of Johnson's new identity. The result was that Johnson did not even need resist because his adversaries' efforts simply had no effect at all. Johnson was behaving so because he was now stable and original. In his expression, he is now living with Africa inside him. He feels that he is now living a new life. The importance of his trip underscores his ability to make positive changes in his new life. He believes that a part of his success will be to set up, someday, a "finding Africa school of thought" for any other "Johnson" that may like to walk out of the encasement of negative identity.

Thinking over his trip to Africa, Johnson said that before his travel to Africa, he needed something strong enough to externalize a problem that would make him admit that he had not done enough to solve his problem. He thinks that not finding an answer to why people from other cultural backgrounds seem to succeed more easily in America while people like him do not or appear to do so with more difficulty did the trick for him. In Africa, he felt a positive change from inside to outside. The change he felt enabled him to believe in himself, and he resolved to do more of whatever it took to solve his problem. He admitted that before he traveled to Africa, it did not come easy for him to identify with Africa, which is not as successful or wealthy as America. Because Johnson achieved what he could not achieve in his life in America in his trip to Africa, he concluded that his regain of originality remains a major value that education or economic success could never have enabled him to achieve. Johnson found Africa. He continues to remember the lessons he learned from the seventy-year-old grandmother and his peers in Ozuzumba.

CHAPTER 10

Johnson, the City Mayor

Americans are generous and strong and decent not because we believe in ourselves, but because we hold beliefs beyond our selves. When this spirit of citizenship is missing, no government program can replace it. When this spirit is present, no wrong can stand against it.

—George W. Bush

After graduation from law school, Johnson secured a job as a prosecutor in a city government. He thought of settling down and worked hard to advance his career. He bought a house as a part of his preparation for starting a family. When Johnson was in law school, he was dating a beautiful white girl named Sarah. After months of dating Johnson, Sarah told her parents she was dating a black guy. Her parents were not much excited about her dating a black guy, and they asked Sarah, "Why a black guy?" Sarah responded, "Why not? He is very smart and educated, and we love each other." Sarah's mother appealed to her husband to take the issue easy with Sarah. Her father slowed down, though he did not seem happy with Sarah. After some hesitation, Sarah's parents asked her to invite Johnson for dinner at their house. Sarah's parents were devoted Christians. So before the date of the dinner, Sarah's parents prayed that God bless her parents to do the right thing, which included the heart with which to accept what they might not like.

On the date appointed for the dinner, Johnson showed up well dressed and looking promising. When Sarah saw Johnson pulling into her parents' driveway, she ran outside to welcome him. They embraced and kissed each other. When Johnson walked into the house, holding hands with Sarah, her parents welcomed Johnson and appeared to like him. However, Sarah's father took time to ask questions to find out as much as possible about Johnson's family background. After some minutes of conversation between Sarah's father and Johnson, Sarah became uncomfortable, feeling that her father was using too many questions to pressure Johnson. But Johnson expected Sarah's parents to ask questions about his background to enable them to get to know him. Johnson remembered the process of marriage contracting in Africa. He remembered that it was the duty of both families involved in a marriage to investigate the background of each other. Johnson said that the purpose of the investigation was actually in his favor. The parents were trying to make sure that the marriage would succeed. In the end, Johnson passed the test and was accepted with open hands by Sarah's parents. This made Sarah very happy.

Johnson took Sarah to his family. Johnson's family asked him, "So you finally went on your way to bring a white woman into our family. How do you expect us to be comfortable in a relationship with a white woman and her family?" Johnson told his family to trust him. "I care about you all, and I will never do anything to hurt any of you," Johnson assured his family that Sarah is a great girl, and her family is even greater. He appealed to his family to bear with him and remember that he came back from Africa as a color-blind person. Johnson sympathized with his family by telling them he knew how they felt. "I was feeling like you all before my trip to Africa," Johnson told his family that his finding Africa made him an original African American. "This made me recapture the original values of the African that came to America as his own master and not as a slave." He reminded them that his return from Africa was like a second coming to America. His trip to Africa put an end to his first coming, and his comeback started a new beginning, a new life, and a new person that is his own master. Johnson said to his family, "Trust me. I have everything under control. Please accept Sarah with all your heart. She is going to be my wife."

Meanwhile, Johnson told Sarah, "We are actually doing what the original founding Fathers of America intended about marriage." He added that the Founding Fathers intended the melting pot to be successful. All people from different cultures were expected to intermarry. The American Fathers believed that when different cultures mix and continue to mix using intermarriages as a design, the product would be a gestalt ethnicity that would be common to all Americans. This vision of the Founding Fathers empowered Johnson and Sarah to see themselves as a typical American couple. Johnson's family then backed down and accepted Sarah. At this point, the minds of both families appeared to meet. Johnson and Sarah started arrangements for their wedding. They threw a party and announced to the public that they were engaged and were getting ready for their wedding. Johnson and Sarah printed and sent their wedding invitation cards to all their friends, especially their friends at law school.

Johnson knew what he wanted. His ambition was to be in politics someday. He used their wedding to create a foundation for their future. He and Sarah used the influence of Sarah's family to invite dignitaries from different works of life to their wedding. Some individuals among the dignitaries saw Johnson as a rising star who could run for office in the future.

Many people helped make Johnson and Sarah's wedding the talk of the town. The wedding was conducted in the most prominent Baptist church in the city. There was a big congregation that went to witness the wedding. The bride and groom, the flower girls, and some friends pulled into the church's parking lot in a limousine for the wedding. A long convoy of cars carrying parents and well-wishers was driving behind the couple's limousine. Of course, there were police escorts in front and behind the convoy. The church wedding ceremony started at exactly 11:00 a.m. When the time for the couple to exchange vows approached, the officiating pastor said to the congregation, "If anybody knows anything that would stop this couple from becoming husband and wife, let him or her say it now." Because nobody said anything or had any objection, the pastor called for the ring bearer. The couple exchanged their vows and rings. The pastor then pronounced the couple husband and wife. The congregation stood up and clapped for them to show support and congratulation.

At the end of the church ceremony, the newlyweds and the congregation walked out of the church, posed for some photographs, and drove to the hotel decorated for the wedding reception. The wedding reception was held in a very prestigious hotel. There was plenty to eat and drink. There was great music, dancing, and merriment. Toward the end of the reception ceremony, the newlyweds were ushered out of the reception hall by family members and friends. The couple took off for their honeymoon at a hotel on an undisclosed island close to America.

When they returned from their honeymoon, they bought a beautiful new home and started building a family. In less than one year, they celebrated the birth of a bouncing baby boy. Johnson applied and was accepted as a member of a prestigious country club. In the meantime, Johnson was doing his job as a prosecutor. In less than two years,

Johnson was promoted to city attorney. He continued to build his popularity in the city. By the following year, the then-mayor announced that he would not be running for reelection. Johnson saw an opportunity to move to the top. He approached several influential people in the city and made known his intention to run for the mayor's office.

Other politicians who were interested in the position of mayor. However, Johnson used the influence of his rich friends to edge out his competitors. Johnson and Sarah campaigned hard for the election. In the end, he built a great organization that helped make his campaign effective. Finally, election day came, and people went to vote to elect a new mayor. After the people had voted, it was late in the evening, and all voting was over. Johnson and his wife and supporters were sitting in their living room, enjoying some refreshments and waiting for the election results. After the votes were counted, a breaking news signal came up on the television: Johnson was announced the winner in the city mayor race. During the campaign, the polls indicated that Johnson would win, but nobody was ever sure of victory until the votes were counted. It turned out that the polls were correct. So after Johnson was announced the city mayor-elect, the celebration started immediately.

Johnson stood in front of the crowd of his supporters and campaign staff, and made an acknowledgment speech. He thanked his staff and supporters and assured the people again of all he promised to do for the city. Johnson was sworn in as city mayor. Johnson's success confirmed what he heard some people say that, indeed, "after thunder comes the rain." Johnson said, "It is true that my ancestors suffered the worst human indignation known to man, but it took their sufferings and sacrifice for me to be born in America and my finding Africa to achieve the American dream. Thanks to the American Constitution that provides freedom and liberty, that enabled me to recover my originality. God bless America."

SHORT PROFILE

Name: Ike Okwuonu

Occupation: mental health therapist

Education: BBA/BS, MA (political science), University of Central Oklahoma; MHR (human relations), University of Oklahoma; doctoral student, University of the Rockies, Colorado Springs